## DATE DUE

| | |
|---|---|
| JUL 25 1985 | NOV 4 1987 |
| DEC 18 1986 | APR 1 1988 |
| APR 14 1986 | SEP 28 1988 |
| APR 28 1986 | MAR 10 1990 |
| JUL 5 1986 | |
| JUL 19 1986 | JUL 1 1991 |
| MAY 19 1987 | SEP 12 1991 |
| MAY 20 1987 | |
| JUN 3 1987 | JUL 14 1993 |
| JAN 27 1989 | JUL 29 1993 |
| | SEP 15 1993 |

# MAGIC BY THE LAKE

*by the same author*

HALF MAGIC

KNIGHT'S CASTLE

THE TIME GARDEN

MAGIC OR NOT?

THE WELL-WISHERS

SEVEN-DAY MAGIC

# Magic by the Lake

EDWARD EAGER

ILLUSTRATED BY N. M. BODECKER

HARCOURT, BRACE & WORLD, INC.
NEW YORK

LIBRARY OF CONGRESS CATALOG CARD NUMBER: 57-5267

PRINTED IN THE UNITED STATES OF AMERICA

FOR CANDACE DRAKE,
my god-daughter and constant reader

# CONTENTS

# CONTENTS

# MAGIC BY THE LAKE

# 1. The Lake

It was Martha who saw the lake first. It was Katharine who noticed the sign on the cottage, and it was Mark who caught the turtle, and it was Jane who made the wish. But it was Martha who saw the lake first. The others didn't see it until at least ten seconds later. Or, as Katharine put it, at long last when all hope was despaired of, the weary, wayworn wanderers staggered into sight of the briny deep.

This, while poetic, was not a true picture of the case. They really weren't so wayworn as all that; the lake was only fifty miles from home. But cars didn't go so fast

3

thirty years ago as they do today; so they had started that morning, their mother and Martha and Mr. Smith their new stepfather in front, and Jane and Mark and Katharine and the luggage in the tonneau, which is what people called the back seat in those days, and Carrie the cat wandering from shoulder to shoulder and lap to lap as the whim occurred to her.

At first spirits were high, and the air rang with popular song, for this was going to be the four children's first country vacation since they could remember. But two hours in a model-T Ford with those you love best *and* their luggage is enough to try the patience of a saint, and the four children, while bright and often quite agreeable, were not saints. It was toward the end of the second hour that the real crossness set in.

"That lake," said Jane, "had better be good when we finally get to it. If ever."

"Are you sure we're on the right road?" said Mark. "That crossroad back there looked better."

"I want to get out," said Martha.

"You can't," said their mother. "Once you start that all pleasure is doomed."

"Then I want to get in back," said Martha.

"Don't let her," said Katharine. "She'll wiggle, and it's bad enough back here already. Sardines would be putting it mildly."

4

"Just cause I'm the youngest, I never get to do anything," said Martha.

"That's right, whine," said Katharine.

"Children," said their mother.

"I," said Mr. Smith, "suggest we stop and have lunch."

So they did, and it was a town called Angola, which interested Mark because it was named after one of the countries in his stamp album, but it turned out not to be very romantic, just red brick buildings and a drugstore that specialized in hairnets and rubber bathing caps and Allen's Wild Cherry Extract. Half an hour later, replete with sandwiches and tasting of wild cherry, the four children were on the open road again.

Only now it was a different road, one that kept changing as it went along.

First it was loose crushed stone that slithered and banged pleasingly underwheel. Then it gave up all pretense of paving and became just red clay that got narrower and narrower and went up and down hill. There was no room to pass, and they had to back down most of the fourth hill and nearly into a ditch to let a car go by that was heading the other way. This was interestingly perilous, and Katharine and Martha shrieked in delighted terror.

The people in the other car had luggage with them, and the four children felt sorry for them, going back to cities and sameness when their own vacation was just beginning. But they forgot the people as they faced the fifth hill.

The fifth hill was higher and steeper than any of the others; as they came toward it the road seemed to go straight up in the air. And halfway up it the car balked, even though Mr. Smith used his lowest gear, and hung straining and groaning and motionless like a live and complaining thing.

"Children, get out," said their mother. So they did.

And relieved of their cloying weight, the car leaped forward and mounted to the brow of the hill, and the four children had to run up the hill after it. That is, Jane and Mark and Katharine did.

Martha was too little to run up the hill. She walked. And nobody gave her a helping hand or waited for her to catch up, and she felt deserted and disconsolate, and the backs of her knees ached. When she arrived at the top, the others were already in the car and urging her on with impatient cries. But she didn't get in the car. She threw herself down among the black-eyed Susans at the side of the road to get her breath. She glanced around. Then she jumped up again.

"Look!" she cried, pointing.

The others looked. Below them and to one side was the lake. They could see only part of it, because land and trees got in the way, but the water lay blue and cool, and there

6

were cattails and water lilies, and from somewhere in the distance came the put-put of a motorboat.

Then Jane and Mark and Katharine started to get back out of the car, and they all clamored to go running right down to the lake now, and take their bathing suits and jump into it.

Mr. Smith had a lenient look in his eye, and their mother must have seen this, for she became firm.

"All in good time," she said. "First things first. Wait till we get to the cottage and unpack."

So Martha climbed back in the car, not feeling out of breath at all any more, and they drove on till they came to a gate. Mark jumped out and opened the gate, and closed it after them, and then they drove over a rolling pasture, and there were sheep staring stupidly and a few rams looking baleful, and then another gate, and beyond it a grove of trees, and in the grove was the cottage.

And of course before there could be any base thought of unloading the car, the four children had to explore every inch of the cottage and the grounds around it, only not going near the water, because their mother's word was law and they kept to the letter of it. But they could see the lake from every window and between the silver birches that picturesquely screened the front.

And naturally there was a hammock slung between two

of the birches, and better still there was a screened porch with cots on it that ran around three sides of the cottage, and that was where the children would sleep. And there were three little rooms with more cots in them downstairs and another cot in a corner of the living room, for rainy nights, only of course there wouldn't be many of those.

There was a big kitchen, and a big room upstairs for their mother and Mr. Smith, and that was all of the cottage.

"I'm sorry it isn't any better," they heard Mr. Smith saying to their mother. "It was the best I could do so late in the season."

The four children couldn't imagine what he meant. So far as they could see, the cottage was all that was ideal.

Next came a horrid interval of unloading and unpacking, but few would wish to hear about that. Suffice it to say that at last the four children emerged in their new bathing suits, and the lake was waiting.

Mark and Katharine were the first to emerge from the cottage. As they waited impatiently for the others, Katharine noticed a sign by the front door. It was of rustic letters made from pieces of tree branch, and they hadn't seen it before because it was the same color as the cottage's brown shingles. "Magic by the Lake," it said.

Katharine looked at Mark, a wild guess in her eyes. "Do

8

you suppose?" For the four children had had experience of magic, or at least a kind of half magic, in the past.

(After the half magic was over, they wondered if they'd ever have any magic adventures again, and in the book about it it says it was a long time before they knew the answer. And here it was only three weeks later, and already Katharine was ready for more. But if you think three weeks isn't a long time for four children to be without magic, I can only say that it seemed a long time to *them*.)

"Could it be going to start again already?" Katharine went on.

Mark shook his head. "Nah," he said. "It's too soon. We couldn't be *that* lucky. That's just one of those goofy names people give things. You know, like 'Dreamicot' and 'Wishcumtrue.' Doesn't mean a thing."

And then Jane and Martha appeared, and their mother and Mr. Smith with them, and there was a race for the small private beach that went with the cottage. And the beach proved to be perfection, first pebbles and tiny snail shells, then soft sand and shallow water for Martha and Katharine, and farther on a diving raft for those like Jane and Mark, who had passed their advanced tests at the "Y" and could swim out deep.

You all know what going swimming is like, and it is even

better when it's your first swim from your own private beach in the first lake you've ever stayed at.

After an hour of bliss, there was the usual rumor among the grownups that maybe they'd been in long enough, and after an hour more even the four children were ready to admit there might be more to life than paddle and splash. Just merely lying in the sun on the sand might be even better. So they did that until their mother cried out and said they would catch their deaths. Then reluctantly they went back to the cottage and put on blue jeans (Mark) and old dresses (the three girls) and set out to explore the rest of the grounds.

They found a nice rustic summerhouse on the high point of the shore that would be useful for sitting in and watching the sunset and listening to the water and the mosquitoes. And down on an inlet, round the corner from the beach, was the boathouse.

The boathouse, when investigated, proved to contain a flat-bottomed rowboat and a trim red canoe named *Lura*, after the first name of Mrs. Kutchaw, from whom they'd rented the cottage. The four children had met Mrs. Kutchaw and did not think Lura an appropriate name for her, but the canoe was dandy. Only their mother, when consulted, said they'd better not take the canoe out without a grownup along, just yet. But the flat-bottomed rowboat they could use, if they were careful.

"Better stay close to shore," said Mr. Smith. "There are parts of this lake in the middle where they've never found bottom."

This impressed the four children very much, and they now had even more respect for the lake than they'd had before. As Mark said, it must be some lake.

None of them had ever done any rowing at all, and of course they all had to try. But after Martha lost an oar and Mark nearly fell in rescuing it, and Katharine almost shipwrecked them on an unhandy sandbank, it was decided that Jane and Mark should take charge, and the other two lay back in luxury and were passengers.

"This is keen," said Mark, after a bit. "I've got the crude inkling of it now, just about."

"I've almost figured out how not to catch crabs already," said Jane, plying the other oar and belying her words by sending a sizable jet of water all over Katharine.

But the shore was slipping by them visibly now, and they explored its possibilities with eager eyes. After their own grove of trees came a cottage or two, then more trees, then more cottages closer together, till up ahead the four children saw a little settlement, with a hotel and a dance pavilion and a soft-drink stand and a pier.

"That must be Cold Springs," said Jane, for that was the unusual name of the resort on this side of the lake.

All the cottages had boats, and most of the boats were

on the water now, and when Mark saw a large excursion launch called the *Willa Mae* heading toward them from the hotel pier, he decided traffic conditions were too difficult for beginners and turned the rowboat around.

So they rowed back along the shore and decided which cottages they liked the looks of, and chose a pink one with curlicues as their favorite, till they came in sight of their own house and beach, already looking familiar and home-like. They rowed round the bend toward the boathouse, but the inlet was so inviting, what with water lilies gleaming whitely, and frogs sitting on lily pads looking bemused, and dragonflies hovering over the water, that Mark and Jane shipped their oars, and the four children drifted gently in the afternoon sun. It was then that Martha saw the turtle swimming past.

It was Mark who caught it. It was a big turtle, and it looked even bigger as he deftly scooped it up and landed it in the bottom of the boat.

"Watch out, maybe it's the snapping kind," said Jane.

But the turtle merely gave one look at the four children and withdrew into its shell in scorn.

"Put it back," said Katharine, who was of a tender heart. "It's not happy here."

"It will be," said Mark. "I'll build it a tank. I'll catch lots more and train them."

But when they had put the boat away and carried the turtle tenderly to the shade of a friendly oak, building a tank right now seemed all too energetic. The four children sat in the shade, lazily eating an occasional gooseberry from a convenient bush, and talked, instead. The turtle still refused to make friends. Its apparently headless, footless shell lay upon the ground nearby.

"This summer," said Katharine, "is going to be a thing of beauty and a joy forever."

"Not quite," said Jane. "It's the middle of July already. Two more months and prison doors will yawn. And I get Miss Martin for seventh grade next year. Help!" And she fell back in a deadly swoon at the thought, and lay pulling up blades of grass and nibbling the juicy white bits off the bottom.

"Why couldn't we have found this place way back at the beginning of vacation?" said Katharine.

"If we had, we wouldn't have found the half-magic charm and Mother wouldn't have got married," said Mark.

"And there wouldn't have been any Uncle Huge to rent a cottage *for* us," said Martha, for that was the charming name she insisted on calling Mr. Smith, whose given name was Hugo.

"Maybe there would have," said Jane. "If I could find a magic charm right on Maplewood Avenue, it stands to reason there must be lots of it lying around still, just waiting for the right person to come along. Meaning me," she added smugly, and whistled through a blade of grass.

"Have you noticed the name on the cottage?" Katharine asked.

Martha and Jane hadn't. Katharine told them.

"Pooh," said Mark. "I told her that doesn't mean a thing. Just a goofy name."

"Maybe it does," said Katharine. "Maybe it means exactly what it says. Maybe there's a secret passage in the wall, and a wishing well, and buried treasure in the cellar!"

"And a dear little fairy in the keyhole," said Mark scoffingly. "Bushwah!"

"Magic by the lake," said Martha, trying out the words to herself. "Doesn't it sound lovely? Don't you wish it *were* true?"

"*I* certainly do," said Jane.

There was a silence. The turtle stuck its head out of its shell.

"Now you've done it," it said.

## 2. The Magic

"What did you say?" said Martha.

"You heard me," said the turtle.

"I didn't know you could talk," said Katharine.

"Well, now you know," said the turtle. And it started to withdraw into its shell again.

"Wait. Please. Don't go," were the words of Katharine and Martha and Jane.

Mark wasted no time in speech. He laid hold of the turtle's head and hung on, deaf to all fear of snappings. The turtle's neck stretched alarmingly, but it could not get free.

16

"I'm sorry if this is uncomfortable," Mark told it politely but firmly. "But you can't just say a thing like that and disappear. You've got to tell us more."

"Oh, very well," said the turtle crossly. "Unloose me," it added in rather a lordly way, and Mark let go its head. "Really, the manners of some people!"

"You're magic," said Martha.

"Naturally," said the turtle. "When a race lives as long as mine does, it stands to reason it would pick up a few rudiments. Of course," it added proudly, "*I* happen to be a particularly intelligent specimen, even for a turtle."

"Can all turtles talk?" asked Katharine.

"Oh, *that!*" said the turtle. "We pick *that* up the first fifty years."

"Why don't you do it oftener then?" said Jane.

"We couldn't be bothered!" snapped the turtle, looking at her with no great liking.

Mark thought it wise to intervene. "About what we were just saying," he said. "Did you mean you've granted our wish?"

"Don't go saying *I* did it!" said the turtle. "Don't come complaining to *me!* People who go around making wishes without looking to see what magic beings are listening can just take the consequences!"

"Oh, we're not complaining," said Katharine quickly.

17

"We think it's awfully nice of you. We're grateful. You've been very obliging. Thank you very much."

"Humph!" said the turtle.

"Magic's just about all we needed to make things just about perfect," said Jane.

"Ha!" said the turtle. "That's what *you* think. And a lot you know about it! But of course you couldn't be sensible, could you, and order magic by the pound, for instance, or by the day? Or by threes, the good old-fashioned way? Or even by halves, the way you did before?"

"Why, how do you know about that?" said Martha.

"I know everything," said the turtle. "If it's worth knowing. But no, not you. You had to be greedy and order magic by the lake, and of course now you've got a whole lakeful of it, and as for how you're going to manage it, I for one wash my hands of the whole question!"

"You mean the whole lake's magic?" said Mark. "*All* of it?"

"It is now," said the turtle.

Jane's eyes turned toward the lake. She gasped. "Look!" she said.

The others looked.

"What did I tell you?" said the turtle. It took one look at the lake, shuddered, and withdrew into its shell.

The four children stared, transfixed.

Every bit of the lake's surface seemed to be suddenly alive, and each bit of it was alive in a different way. It was like trying to keep track of a dozen three-ring circuses, only more so.

Water babies gamboled in the shallows. A sea serpent rose from the depths. Some rather insipid-looking fairies flew over. A witch hobbled on a far bank. A rat and a mole and a toad paddled along near the willowy shore, simply messing about in a boat. A family of dolls explored a floating island. On the other side of the same island, a solitary man stared at a footprint in the sand. A hand appeared in the middle of the lake holding a sword. Britannia ruled the waves. Davy Jones came out of his locker. Neptune himself appeared, with naiads and Nereids too numerous to mention.

The two younger children shut their eyes.

"Make it stop," said Martha.

"Now I know what too much of a good thing means," said Katharine. "I never thought there could be before."

"I wouldn't enjoy it," said Jane, surveying the lake critically. "Not in front of all those people. We couldn't enter in."

"Maybe it could be sort of simplified," said Mark. "Moderation is pleasant to the wise." And he turned to appeal to the turtle.

But the turtle had seized this opportunity to escape and was making for the water as fast as it could, which was fortunately not very fast.

The four children gave chase and brought it to bay. It went into its shell again. Mark rapped on the shell politely. The turtle peered cautiously from within.

"We've got to talk this over," said Mark. "You've got to do something."

"I did," said the turtle, from inside the shell, "and now look! There's no satisfying some people. And you needn't go asking me to take it back, because it's too late. Magic has rules, you know, the same as everything else."

"Yes, we know," said Mark, "but you'd never think so, to look at it now. It's all every which way."

They all looked at the lake again. Some Jumblies had appeared, going to sea in a sieve. A walrus and a carpenter danced with some oysters on a nearby shore. In the distance Columbus was discovering America.

"It's too big," said Katharine. "I think it needs alterations."

"Couldn't you let us have a few more wishes," said Jane, "so we can sort of tame it and know where we stand?"

"We'll be awfully grateful," said Katharine. "We'll build you a lovely tank and give you the best care money can buy."

"No, thank you," said the turtle. "I was perfectly happy in my own inlet, until you came along. I had a lovely life there. I want to go home."

"Not till you let us make more wishes," said Jane, putting her foot on the turtle firmly.

"Oh, very well," said the turtle, "if I must, I must. Only *I* have to make them. *I'm* the magic one around here. And only three, mind. That's the magic number."

"Naturally," said Jane.

"Proceed," said the turtle. Jane removed her foot.

"First of all," said Mark, who had been thinking, "let's have only one magic adventure at a time. And not every day, just every so often. Then we'll have time to recover in between."

"Is that all one wish?" said the turtle. "I'll try, but it will take a lot out of me. The other two had better be easy."

"No grownups noticing," said Katharine. "So Mother won't abandon all hope of sanity, the way she did last time."

"And nothing scary," said Martha.

"Granted," said the turtle, "and that is absolutely *all*."

The other three turned on Martha. "What did you have to go and ask *that* for?" said Jane. "Now it'll be all tame and namby-pamby and watered down! Like those awful children's editions of books Aunt Grace always gives us!"

"That *Three Musketeers* with Lady de Winter left right *out!*" said Mark.

21

"Excavated versions, I think they're called," said Katharine. "You can see why."

The turtle gave them a look. "Don't be so sure," it said. "After all, *I* made the wish; so there won't be anything in it that would scare *me*. But then," it added, and Katharine swore afterwards that it winked at them, "nothing *does!*"

And it started for the lake, leaving the four children with that to think over.

Mark ran after it. "Wait," he said. "How'll we know when it's time?"

"You won't," said the turtle, turning at the water's edge. "When you feel like magic, touch the lake and wish, and if the time is ripe, you'll get it. Or not, as the case may be." And it plopped into the water.

"Will we see you again?" Jane called.

"Not if I see you first," were the parting words of the turtle. "Try not to call unless it's absolutely necessary." And it swam away.

And where it touched the water, the magic started disappearing, and the disappearing spread outwards to both sides, like the wake of a ship, until, as the last ripple of turtle vanished in the distance, the lake lay calm and untroubled and uninhabited (except in a normal fishy way) under the setting sun, just as though nothing out of the ordinary had happened.

"So that's that," said Jane, "and we're left to cope with it."

"When'll it start, do you suppose?" said Katharine.

"Tonight?" faltered Martha. "We just touched the lake a while back, and I was probably wishing all sorts of things."

"I shouldn't think so," said Mark. "I shouldn't think till tomorrow, when it's fresh. It's getting pretty late now."

"Good," said Martha. "I'd rather it didn't start at night."

"Joy cometh in the morning," said Katharine.

"Dinner!" called their mother.

The four children went into the cottage.

Going to bed that night was interesting, for they had never slept on their own sleeping porch before, to say nothing of crickets, and water softly lapping, and the sound that night in the country makes, which really isn't a sound at all but the echo of silence.

"The end of a perfect day," said Mark, from his side of the porch.

"Peace, perfect peace," said Jane, from hers.

On the long front part, by the summerhouse and the silver birches, Martha got out of her bed and into Katharine's.

"What's the matter? Can't you sleep?" said Katharine.

"I keep thinking," said Martha. "I keep thinking about

23

all that magic in the lake. And that part where they've never found bottom. And that big snake thing that came up out of it."

"Trust ye unto the magic's power," called Jane, who had overheard. "It never let us down before."

"In youth it sheltered us," said Katharine. "Chances are it'll protect us now."

At that moment a bloodcurdling laugh rent the air.

"Help! What was that?" said Jane.

"A loon," said Mark, who was a Boy Scout.

"What's a loon?" whispered Martha, trembling.

"A bird," Katharine told her.

"It couldn't be," said Martha. "It's that big snake thing."

"Hush," said Katharine. "Listen to the crickets."

"I don't like them," said Martha. "They could be ghosts twittering."

"They aren't," said Katharine. "Get back in your own bed."

"Hold my hand, then," said Martha.

"Oh, all right," said Katharine.

And Martha got back in her own bed, and Katharine reached out an arm from *hers*, and the sisters joined hands in the space between. And which limp hand fell first from the lifeless clasp of the other and sank into utter drowsiness will never be known. The next thing that *was* known was the sun shining in their eyes and turning the lake all blue and gold.

Breakfast followed as the day the night, and then Mr. Smith had to leave for the city in time to open the bookshop for the afternoon, which is what he had decided to do every day this summer except week ends, when he would be gloriously free, like the others. But first he drove the four children over the rolling pasture to a farm on the red clay road, and they saw milk being milked, and carried the nourishing cans of it back to the car; and today Mr. Smith delivered it and them to the cottage, but after this getting the milk would be the four children's morning task, on foot.

And then Mr. Smith departed, and the children's mother suggested a morning dip.

Farms have charms to soothe the most savage breast, and swimming is just about the highest good; so it was some time before thoughts of magic entered the children's heads. When they touched the lake for the first time, all they wished was that swimming would be as wonderful today as it was yesterday, and it was.

It wasn't till they lay spent on the sand that they began wondering about the magic, and when it would begin, and what would be its alluring form when it did.

"Do you suppose we get to sort of choose at all, or will it take us by surprise?" said Jane.

"Shush," said Katharine, nodding in the direction of their mother, who was sitting all too nearby.

But their mother didn't look up from the book she was reading and didn't appear to have heard a word; so that part of the magic seemed to be working already.

"What would everybody choose if we could?" said Jane.

"Pirates," said Mark at once, touching the edge of lake that rippled shallowly at his feet.

"Mermaids," said Katharine, touching *her* bit of lake-edge at the same moment.

"Neither one," said Martha quickly, but nobody heard her because everybody was talking at once.

"That's done it," Mark said. "Now I suppose we'll get a sort of blend."

"What would the blend of a mermaid and a pirate be?" said Jane.

"A mer-pirate," said Katharine. "Long golden hair and black whiskers."

But that wasn't what the four children saw a few minutes later. What they saw, floating toward the beach, was a perfectly ordinary mermaid, such as you might meet any day in any perfectly ordinary sea. She was combing her long golden hair, and the scales of her supple tail glittered through the foam behind her. She saw the four children and beckoned with her golden comb.

26

"Come, dear children, let us away, down and away below," were her thrilling words.

Martha chose this moment to be difficult, as only she knew how.

"I won't go," she said. "I know all about what she does. Mother read me a story. She lures poor sailors, and they drown. Something about a laurel eye."

Jane propelled her sister forward. "You can't back out now," she said, "now we're in the thick of it."

"It would be changing courses in the middle of the stream," said Katharine.

"Then that's what I'll do," said Martha.

But Jane took hold of one of her arms and Mark took hold of the other, and Katharine pushed from behind, and the mermaid seemed to take hold of all of them, though she had only two hands, and they shot forward into the lake.

"Mother!" called Martha, to the vanishing shore.

"I see you," her mother nodded smilingly. "Keep it up; you're swimming fine."

Martha's answering wail was cut short as the waters closed over her head.

At first she kept her eyes tight shut, but at last fear gave way to curiosity, and she opened them cautiously. To her surprise she could see perfectly well under water, which had never been true before, but she couldn't see much, because they were going too fast. She got an impression of sandy bottom far below. Things moved squidgily in it, and Martha shut her eyes again firmly.

Katharine was holding her breath. After a while she began to wonder if this were absolutely necessary. At last, when utter bursting seemed likely, she decided to try.

"Can we breathe, do you suppose?" she said, "or will we drown?"

"Glug glug," were the words of Mark. Or at least that's what they sounded like. Katharine decided that breathing was possible but conversation wasn't.

Then, just as the rushing wateriness was beginning to pall on even the most venturesome heart (Jane's), there was a change in the atmosphere. It grew lighter, and brighter, and next thing the four children shot out of it entirely into open air.

"Land ahoy!" said Mark.

"Where are we?" said Martha, relieved to find herself anywhere.

Jane's eyes were shining. "Lagoons!" she said, pointing. "Desert islands. Coral reefs. Coves."

The others looked where she pointed. There was only one island and one coral reef and one lagoon (or cove), but that was exciting enough. They were floating rapidly past the reef and into the lagoon and toward the island, the mermaid (who seemed to be a mermaid of few words) still towing them.

Then they touched land, and barnacles scraped Katharine's knee.

"I didn't know the lake had all this in it," she said. "Which way is home?"

"Don't be silly," said Mark. "We left that old lake behind ages ago. We're halfway around the world by now. Feel the climate. It's tropical."

Jane was already scrambling up the rocks. Mark hoisted Martha up to her, and he and Katharine followed. The mermaid draped herself fishily against the base of the rock.

"So far, so good," she said. "Now sing."

"Sing what?" said Katharine.

"What for?" said Mark.

"To lure a ship in to shore, of course, stupid," said the mermaid.

"What did I tell you?" said Martha.

But now the mermaid was raising her voice in song, and Jane and Katharine, feeling that in a magic adventure it is best to do whatever seems to be expected of you, joined in. After a bit, Martha added her piping tones to theirs.

Who knows what song the sirens sang? I do not, and neither did Sir Thomas Browne, who once wrote some well-known lines on the subject. Few will ever know what song Jane and Katharine and Martha sang upon that coral coast, either.

But they listened to the mermaid's tune and did their best to follow it, and as to what words they sang, they let inspiration take its course. "Come unto these yellow sands," they sang. "Come all ye young fellows who follow the sea. Come, come, I love you only; my heart is true."

Katharine even tried to put in the alto, the way her Aunt Grace always did in church. As for Jane, she got carried away completely, and soon was nodding and becking and smiling wreathed smiles, and waving her freckled arms with alluring grace, and combing her longish un-golden hair with the mermaid's extra comb, which she borrowed for the purpose.

Mark, who had been holding his ears, turned away and made a gagging sound.

But the song seemed to do the trick, for a sail appeared on the horizon and turned into a ship that veered from its course and came rapidly toward them. And as it came nearer, a delighted gasp was heard from the four children, and they would have shivered happily in their shoes, except that they didn't have any on, being still dressed for swimming.

For the ship was dark and looming, and its sails were

black and sinister. A skull and crossbones was its suitable flag. And among the toiling figures on the deck walked a tall man in high boots and the kind of hat that made it all too plain what his dreadful trade was, and from the way he strutted up and down you could tell even at a distance that he thought it was a glorious thing to be a pirate king.

"Shiver my timbers!" said Jane.

"Shush," said Mark.

The ship was so near now that the four children could hear the pirate's voice plainly as he gave orders to drop anchor and man the longboat. A few seconds later the longboat began to descend.

"This is where I leave you," said the mermaid, in a businesslike way. And without a backward glance she turned tail and sank beneath the waves.

"Wait!" cried Katharine, for there was much she wanted to ask the mermaid about life in undersea circles.

But the mermaid was gone, and the four children were left a prey to feelings of doubt and conspicuousness as the pirate chief and his men drew ever nearer to shore in the longboat.

"Let's hide," said Martha suddenly, and all agreed that the suggestion was excellent.

The island afforded little shelter except palm trees, but the four children were soon stationed behind four of these, all too aware of the fact that their plumper parts were still sticking out plainly to either side of the meager trunks.

The bow of the longboat ground against sand, and the pirate chief leaped nimbly ashore, for all his high, heavy boots. The children could see that he was a handsome devil, with beautifully curling black whiskers.

"Up with the treasure and after me," he said to his men. "Bring spades, picks, and shovels."

Some of the men heaved a great chest up out of the boat. Others followed with the tools of digging. The black-whiskered one strode to a sandy spot just in front of the four palm trees. He pointed with his fine, white, gentlemanly hand that had rings on all the fingers, diamonds and emeralds.

"Dig," he said.

And the men dug long and deep in the sand, while their chief paced up and down, muttering to himself and biting his nails. He did not seem to see the four children, though they were sure that any minute he would.

"This treasure," he muttered, "will rest safely here till I am ready to retire and take my place in the world as a gentleman, or my name's not Chauncey Cutlass!"

One of the digging men had overheard, and whispered to his fellows. They put down their spades. The first man stepped forward, with the others behind him. "What about our part in it?" he said. "We pirated it the same as you."

"Can't they see us?" hissed Jane, from behind her tree.

"I guess not," Mark hissed back. "Kathie wished grown-ups wouldn't notice, and I guess the..."

same as...

The men gro...

"Well, all right, then," sa...

The men dug again.

Katharine, like many a more classic heroine before her, chose this moment to sneeze.

The pirates jumped. So did the four children.

"Hark!" said Chauncey Cutlass. "What was that?"

There was a pause. Then Mark proved what a hero he could be, if necessary. He stepped out from behind his palm tree.

"It was me," he started to say. But he suppressed the words in time. For Chauncey Cutlass and his men were looking straight at him, and yet they seemed to be looking straight through him at the horizon beyond.

" 'Twas nothing," said Cutlass, after a moment. "Mayhap a sea gull flying over."

"A black-tailed godwit, I'd say," said a learned pirate, "or a booby."

"Or a seal barking," said another.

"But they're magic," Katharine joined in the whispering. "They ought to notice *everything*. You'd think."

"I guess they *kind* of notice, but not much," whispered Mark.

"How the wind whispers in the trees," said Chauncey Cutlass, just to prove it.

"This is dandy," said Jane. "Now we can plague them and prey on them and bamboozle them to our heart's content, and they'll never know who. What could be sweeter?"

"What'll we do?" said Katharine.

"Let's not do anything," said Martha.

"Hurry up with that digging," said Chauncey Cutlass to his men, "and back to the ship. I like not this shore. The very trees seem to be staring at me, and the air seems full of voices. Spirits, I suppose. Still, all the better to guard the treasure with. Now. In with the box."

The digging men stopped digging and heaved the treasure chest down and into the hole. Then they started to shovel the earth in on top of it.

"Heel it down firmly," said Chauncey Cutlass, and they

did, with a flat stone on top to mark the spot. Then the elegant pirate ordered one of the men to spread a cloak on the ground so he wouldn't soil his own velvet knees. And he knelt down and carved his initials on the stone with a diamond from one of his rich rings.

The four children meanwhile had repaired to the long-boat, and the others were soothing the faltering Martha, who wanted to steal the boat now while all backs were turned and row away with it. And she wasn't interested in staying to play tricks on the pirates, either.

"It wouldn't be right," she said. "What did they ever do to us?"

"Honestly!" said Jane. "Imagine bringing up a thing like that at a time like this! Pointing morals when you're really just scared! They're *pirates!* They *ought* to be preyed on! It's the Golden Rule!"

"Yes, I suppose there *is* that," said Martha.

"Don't worry," said Mark. "We've had lots fearfuller adventures than this and lived to tell the tale."

"That's true," said Martha. She wrestled with her fears for a minute, then set her jaw grimly. "All right," she said. "It's war to the teeth."

"Good," said Jane.

And now Chauncey Cutlass had finished his carving and strode to the shore, and his men clambered after him.

The four children barely had time to jump into the long-boat before it was pushed off.

Inside the boat it was rather crowded, what with four extra passengers. "Stop shoving," said Captain Cutlass to Simon Sparhatch.

"I ain't," said Sparhatch.

"This is lovely," said Katharine, who was squashed between them. "Like being invisible, only better!" And she nudged the captain in the ribs with her elbow.

"Don't be so familiar," said the captain, glaring at Sparhatch haughtily.

"I bain't," said Sparhatch.

"Careful," said Mark to Katharine. "Don't do anything rash till we get on the ship. Once aboard the lugger and the world is ours."

"Maybe we can scuttle it with all hands," said Martha, her eyes glowing. That was always the way with Martha. Once she stopped being a baby she could be the terror of the block and the fiercest of any of them. Mark only hoped she wouldn't go too far, now she was roused.

They drew nearer to the ship, and the children could read its chilling name, *The Scourge of Cuba*.

"Yo ho," said Jane, "for the Spanish Main."

"Pieces of eight," muttered Martha.

The pirates climbed the rope ladder to the deck, but the

four children lolled luxuriously in the longboat and waited for the pirates to hoist them aboard.

"Summat be ailing with this here boat," said one of the pirates who were doing the hoisting. "It be heavy as a old scow."

" 'Tis bewitched," said Simon Sparhatch, who was helping him. " 'Tis them island spirits still a-following of us. Sure 'tis a cursed voyage. There be a Jonah aboard, and scrape my barnacles if it be not the captain hisself, the great strutting popinjay!"

"Stow it, Sparhatch," said the other pirate. "That be mutinous talk."

"Then let it be," said Sparhatch, making the boat fast.

This gave Mark an idea. Maybe if they could stir the men up enough, then maybe they would have a mutiny as *well* as a pirate ship, and who could ask for anything more? As they scrambled out of the longboat onto the deck, he called the others around him in a whispering huddle.

They made a few quick plans and then separated, Mark hurrying forward to the captain's cabin, while the three others ran to the mainmast. Coming from inland and being mere girls besides, they knew little of nautical matters, but Katharine untied all the knots she could see, and Jane found a jackknife and cut a few ropes here and there, and the sails were soon sagging and flopping and tangling with each other like wet sheets that you try to hang out on the line on a windy washday.

"Sink me!" cried one of the pirates, looking up. "What devil's wind is this, fouling our rigging while the sea be all calm as glass and nary a breeze stirring?"

"Sure the ship be haunted!" cried another.

Katharine located the line that controlled the skull-and-crossbones flag and started to let it down, and a moan went up from the deck.

"Wurra wurra!" cried all the pirates. "We be all doomed! See the flag standing at half-mast for the whole crew of us!"

As for Martha, she knew no bounds. "Pinch them, fairies, black and blue!" she cried. And running among the pirates, she suited the action to the words. The pirates began howling with fear and swatting at the air, and one or two even climbed the rail, ready to plunge overboard and escape the ghostly pinches.

"Belay!" cried Simon Sparhatch, taking command of the panicking men. "The doom need be for only one of us! And who but that great fop of a captain who landed us on that cursed island and catched us this swarm of spirits in the first place? Over the side with him and rid us of these pinching pests!" And he snatched up a belaying pin and started for the captain's cabin.

All the pirates ran along after him, with cries of "Mutiny! Keelhaul him! Down among the dead men!" And Jane and Katharine and Martha ran with the others.

Meanwhile, Mark had stealthily entered the captain's cabin and looked around. The captain was standing before a mirror curling his black whiskers with an iron and admiring his reflection. Mark stole up behind him, removed the brace of pistols from his belt, gave them a good dousing with the captain's own Eau de Cologne, and replaced them. The captain didn't seem to notice, exactly, but an uneasy expression crossed his countenance.

"Am I alone?" he said to the air. "I thought I was alone."

Mark closed the door behind him. "Now we can have a really good talk," he said.

The captain didn't seem to hear the words, exactly, but he saw the door closing, and his proud face blanched.

"Whose ghost are you?" he said. "Are you Horrible Herbert that I fed to the sharks in Biscay Bay or Newgate Ned that I marooned and left to die on Rumtoddy Reef?"

"Beware!" said Mark in a hollow voice. And whether or not the word was heard, the sense of it got across. Chauncey Cutlass trembled.

"Your ship is adrift, and your men have mutinied," said Mark. "You are as good as shark-bait, yourself, already!" And the shouts of the mutinying crew were heard outside the door to prove it.

Chauncey Cutlass showed that, whatever else he was, he had courage. He flung the door open and fired point-blank at Simon Sparhatch, who was in the lead. But a damp and perfumy puff of smoke was all that issued from the pistol.

"Ha!" said Sparhatch, sniffing the air. "His powder be like himself, a great fizzle! A fitting ammunition for a mincing jackanapes! Up with him to the deck and toss the dainty dancing-master over the rail, then away to Hispaniola to make our fortune!"

The captain was trundled up the companionway, and villain though he was, the four children could not help feeling sorry for him, a victim of that merciless crew of cutthroats.

But they reckoned without the craft and courage of Chauncey Cutlass.

"Avast!" he cried, as the sailors lifted him to the rail. "If you drop me, I swear by the Great Horn Spoon I'll come back and haunt you worse than these others! A plague on you for a bunch of mollycoddles, letting some old ghosts ruin our whole cruise! If you do as I say, we'll be free of the pesky things sooner than you can box the compass! If we can feel their pinches, surely we can feel to *catch* them, or I'm a swab and a landlubber!"

The crew fell back and hesitated before him.

"Quick!" he went on, jumping lightly down from the

rail. "Batten down all hatches so none may escape from the deck. Then form two parties, and all in each party join hands. Stretch out the width of the deck. Start at the stern and let one party stalk them to starboard and the other to port. When the two parties meet, you should have them trapped between you!"

Cowed by his fierce glance, the men obeyed, though Simon Sparhatch sulked and muttered.

And a horrible sort of game followed, as the pirates stalked the deck, feeling before them and hunting down the spirit-like children, who fled vainly from one line only to encounter the other.

"Here's one," cried a pirate, laying hold of Jane. "A fierce female ghost, to judge by the hair and teeth."

"And here be another," said a second pirate, poking at Martha experimentally. "A small fat one."

"Why, you!" said Martha, outraged.

Katharine was caught after that, and Mark last of all.

"Beware!" Mark cried balefully, as before, but this time Chauncey Cutlass was beyond frightening.

"I don't care whose ghosts you are!" he said. "I'll teach you to come haunting *me!* Fetch a plank and let them walk it. Then we'll see whether ghosts can swim!"

A plank was fetched, and the four children pushed onto it by the feel-and-grab method. Though invisible to the pirates, they were all too evident to each other, and none took comfort from the pale cheeks of the others.

"Will we drown, do you suppose?" said Jane. "We didn't before."

"Then we had a personally conducted mermaid," Katharine reminded her.

"Now, if ever," said Mark, "is time to call the turtle. It said not unless it was absolutely necessary, and it is."

"Here, turtle," said Martha.

"That's no way," said Mark. "It's not just some old pet. You want to be respectful, and flatter it. O turtle," he began. But at that moment Chauncey Cutlass signaled to the men to tilt the plank, and his words ended in wetness.

There was a moment of doubt, and struggling, and lashing out, and courage sinking to its lowest ebb. Then a familiar voice sounded in Mark's ear.

"Well?" it said. "Pirates were what you asked for. I hope you're satisfied."

Mark opened his eyes. A familiar figure was swimming beside him. But there seemed to be three more figures just like it, only smaller, swimming there, too. And suddenly Mark realized that he felt very peculiar and stiff in the middle and small in the arms and legs.

"What happened?" he said.

"Didn't you ever hear of turning turtle?" said the turtle. "It was the only thing I could think of at the time."

43

Mark looked down at himself. It was true. Plated shells encased him on top and below, and little fat arms and legs protruded from the corners and were paddling him along through the water.

"Now," said the turtle, "you can see how the other half lives."

"Thanks," said Mark.

They went on swimming. They went on swimming for what seemed like forever, for turtles are not the quickest of creatures, but at last they came into shallow water and up over the familiar sand and pebbles and snail shells of their own beach.

"There," said the turtle. And it swam away, leaving the other four turtles on the shore, confidently waiting to change back to their real selves.

But they didn't.

Not a thing happened except that their mother looked up from her book and said, "Well, did you have a good swim? Come on inside; it's time for lunch."

And she went into the cottage, and the four turtles looked at each other, and shrugged, which is hard to do when you are a turtle, and plodded after her.

Carrie the cat took one look at them, hissed, spat, and leaped onto the mantel. But their mother went on not noticing a thing, except to scold them for tracking water

44

into the house and tell them to go back outside and dry themselves.

Handling a Turkish towel is even harder for a turtle than shrugging, and sitting at the table to eat lunch was harder yet, particularly as it was turtle soup.

"I feel like a cannibal," said Katharine.

"Cheer up. Maybe it's just mock," said Mark.

"What do turtles eat usually?" said Martha.

"Fish eggs, don't they?" said Jane. "Do we have any caviar?"

"Certainly not," said their mother. "What in the world are you talking about?"

After lunch she took them for a walk to Cold Springs to buy a few necessaries of life, and the four turtles caused quite a stir among the lakeside children as they stood in the grocery-store cashier's line carrying their parcels. But of course none of the grownups noticed anything unusual, and scolded all their children roundly when they got home for telling such horrid pointless fibs. Several were sent to bed without any supper.

As for Jane and Mark and Katharine and Martha's mother, she didn't seem to see the other children crying out and pointing, but got quite cross at her own offspring for the way they were dilly-dallying and walking so slowly today. The four turtles grew wearier and wearier and more and more footsore as they plodded homeward, trying to keep up with her.

It was with feelings of utter exhaustion that they finally flopped on the cool grass under the hammock late that afternoon. Martha went so far as to withdraw into her shell and announce that she wasn't coming out until conditions improved.

"How long will it last, do you suppose?" said Katharine.

"Till sundown, I guess, if it's like all the books," said Mark, "though this isn't like any book I ever read."

"The shell part's the worst," said Jane. "My middle keeps itching, and I can't get at it to scratch."

At that moment the sun sank redly behind the silver birches, and a few seconds later Katharine smiled with relief at the ordinary, but welcome, face of her older sister. Martha uncurled her head and arms and legs from a very peculiar and uncomfortable-looking position.

"After this," said Mark, "I'm going to feel lots closer to that turtle. Think what it goes through."

"I shouldn't think it would put up with it," said Jane. "I should think it'd go on strike."

"We must be specially kind to it," said Katharine, "when we see it again."

"I wonder when we will," said Martha.

"Dinner," said their mother, from the doorway.

And they went inside.

46

## 3. The Canoe

"The thing is," said Mark, after their morning swim next day, "how often does every so often *come*? We said not every day; so at least today'll be time out."

"That doesn't signify," said Katharine. "We asked it to give us time to rest up, in between, and I'm all rested now."

"Who isn't?" said Jane.

"Me," said Martha, but of course nobody paid any attention to *her*.

"The turtle said when we feel like magic we should touch the lake and wish, and if the time is ripe, we'll get it," Mark reminded them.

"Well?" said Jane. "What are we waiting for? Lake, here we come. What does everybody want to wish? Now *I* think," she started to go on.

"If you ask *me*," said Katharine at the same time.

"*My* idea is," said Mark.

A period of utter confusion and rude interrupting followed. But at last Jane and Katharine and Mark decided that being in on the burning of Rome was what would make this morning just about perfect.

Martha said she didn't feel like going anywhere or seeing anything right now, let alone a burning, and anyway their mother had said never to play with fire, and anyway she wasn't going to come. And she started burying herself in the sand, all but her head, "like an ostrich, only backwards," as Katharine said.

"Never mind her. Come on," said Jane. So she and Mark and Katharine went down to the water's edge and touched the lake and wished. They waited, but nothing happened.

"I guess the time's still green," said Katharine.

"Yes," said Mark. "I kind of figured it might be. It stands to reason. We don't want to be greedy."

"We ought to have sort of a timetable, though," said Jane. "Like every third day or something. Something we can depend on. This way's too risky. It'd be just like that magic to sneak up behind us when we least want it."

"Let's find the turtle and ask," said Katharine.

To board the flat-bottomed rowboat was but the work of a moment, and a moment after *that* Jane and Mark and Katharine were cruising round the inlet among the frogs and the lily pads. Turtles were there in abundance on every side, but who was to say which was *their* turtle?

"O turtle?" said Mark experimentally to the nearest one. It took one look at the four children, turned, and swam away as fast as it could.

"Was that him or not?" said Katharine ungrammatically. "I thought ours was more sort of pointy."

"What's the difference?" said Jane. "Let it go. Our turtle said *all* turtles are magic, didn't it? All we need to do is row up near any one of them and wish it would start granting wishes. If we could get two or three of them working for us at once, we could have wishes practically every few minutes!"

"No, that wouldn't be right," said Mark. "It'd be going against the rules, I know it would. It wouldn't be fair."

"Who cares?" said Jane ruthlessly. "We can be the exception that improves the rule." She raised her voice. "I wish," she began.

Immediately there was a plopping sound from all sides as all the turtles in the neighborhood jumped into the water and swam rapidly away before they could hear any more. So that seemed to be that.

"Oh, well," said Mark. "We've still got the lake, magic or not." And Jane and Katharine had to agree.

They tied the boat to a convenient willow tree and went and dug Martha out of the sand and threw her into the shallow water to wash her off. Then they all jumped in after her and had another swim. Then it was time to get dressed for lunch. And after lunch their mother sent them to Cold Springs to get the mail.

Getting the mail was lots more fun at Cold Springs than it ever had been at home, with none of your ordinary mailmen or post office boxes, exciting as these may be at times, like Christmas, for instance.

Cold Springs managed these things much more interestingly.

At exactly one o'clock every day a truck came whizzing up and stopped between the hotel and the dance pavilion. And a hoarse-voiced lady in a red straw hat stood in the back of the truck and cried out the names on the different pieces of mail, and everybody stood around listening, and those whose mail it was spoke up and claimed it.

Today the four children stood up in the crowd and listened admiringly while the hoarse lady shrieked, "Yagerfritz! Spooncraft! Iggleblod!" Or perhaps those weren't quite the names, but that's what they sounded like.

"I wish we'd get an interesting package, don't you?" said Katharine to Martha.

"Don't!" Martha almost screamed. "Suppose the time got to be ripe suddenly and it came true? We might get a ticking one with a bomb inside!"

"I haven't touched the lake, silly," said Katharine.

"You have so," said Martha. "You were lazy and left your bathing suit on under your dress; I saw you. It's still damp, and there's lake water touching you right now."

Katharine looked down. Sure enough, a damp patch showed through her dress at her middle.

At that moment the hoarse lady called out the four children's last name. Everybody gasped. Mark took the package gingerly. But it turned out to be just the extra blue jeans their mother had ordered for him, and all agreed that, while useful, they could hardly be called interesting.

Katharine got a letter from her best friend Edie Eubank, and that was all the mail. Edie was enthralling in her description of life at home during the one day the children had been gone. The Loo Tay Hand Laundry had burned down, and Edie had caught seventeen grasshoppers and put them in a bottle, and she was yours friendly, Edie Eubank. By the time Katharine had finished reading the letter out loud, the four children were back at the cottage.

For the rest of the afternoon they went their several ways. Martha started making a collection of snail shells from the beach, and Katharine caught grasshoppers and put them in a bottle, to be like Edie Eubank, only she was tender-hearted and let them out again every time she had two or three gathered together.

Mark lay in the hammock reading *By Pike and Dike*.

Only Jane, ever the most persistent, put her time to good employ by making a list of interesting wishes to be wished. She started with suitably watery things, like diving twenty thousand leagues under the sea and getting caught in a typhoon and crossing the Pacific Ocean in an aeroplane (for few people had done that in those days).

But as the afternoon wore on, she branched out and put down just anything exciting that occurred to her. Pretty soon Mark came over to the summerhouse, where she was sitting, and started reading over her shoulder (and breathing down her neck).

"Besiege a castle. Explore Mars. Be a movie star," he read. And then down at the bottom of the page, "rabbit hole?" written with a question mark after it and then crossed out.

"What's that mean?" he said.

Jane blushed. "Oh, that. That's nothing. That's dumb. When I was little, I always kind of wanted to be a rabbit in a rabbit hole. That's kid stuff, though."

"Sure." Mark was sympathetic. "And if we did it, that would be bound to be the day a fox came hunting round." But all the same it made him feel good about Jane somehow to think that she could have ideas like that, and not just be bold and dashing *all* of the time. "Being otters might not be so bad," he said. "They have lots of fun, sliding down those old slides. It'd be handy to the lake, too."

And then the chug-a-chug of Mr. Smith's car was heard, and Mark ran to open the gate and let him in from the field.

Mr. Smith seemed tired at dinner, as well he might, for driving fifty miles twice a day wasn't so easy back in those earlier days of motoring. He seemed a bit worried, too, and said business at the bookshop hadn't been too good today. But he perked up after dinner and asked whether everybody would like to go up to Cold Springs for a while. For at Cold Springs there was dancing in the pavilion three nights a week, and this was one of the nights.

Even as he spoke, the strains of distant music came wafting down the lake, with that extra haunting beauty that music heard over the water always has, and from that moment on all was spatter and dash as the girls did the dinner dishes and everybody hurried into good clothes and rummaged for extra flashlights. Twenty minutes later the procession started, going single file because the path was narrow.

Walks in the country at night are always mysterious, and

53

land that may be friendly and familiar by day seems suddenly strange and untamed. Tonight their own grove of trees was a haunted forest and their lake a vast unexplored sea, hanging dark and cavernous at their elbow. The silver birches glimmered like ghosts. The four children were glad when they passed a lighted cottage.

But soon there were more lights up ahead, and the noise and bustle of Cold Springs. And the dance orchestra, which had taken time out for Orange Crushes, began playing again, and they entered the pavilion to the triumphant strains of "Tiger Rag."

Mr. Smith bought a whole strip of dance tickets at ten cents each, and he and the children's mother danced. He offered some tickets to the four children, but Mark shuddered at the very thought and quickly lost himself in a crowd that was buying cotton candy, and Jane and Katharine were too proud to dance with each other.

"What are we, mere wallflowers?" said Jane haughtily.

So they and Martha sat and watched the dancers, and pretty soon Mark joined them and treated them all to cotton candy, to make amends.

It was interesting studying the lovely young girls and their white-flanneled escorts and deciding which were the prettiest (or handsomest) and criticizing their dresses and dancing form. At least, it was interesting to Jane and Katharine.

"Cheek-to-cheek!" said Jane, pointing to a couple that was dancing in that picturesque position. "*I* think it's disgusting!"

"Romantic, though," said Katharine dreamily.

Mark uttered a sound of contempt. What interested Mark was a sign prominently displayed on the dance floor. "Shimmy-Sha-Wobble Positively Prohibited," it said. He hoped that pretty soon somebody would do the Shimmy-Sha-Wobble, whatever that might be, and be put off the floor. But nobody did, and he began to yawn, a prey to restlessness.

Martha was openly bored, and went and climbed up on the bandstand and talked to the piano player, and kept asking him to play "Yes, We Have No Bananas," which was the only popular song she knew, until he told her to go away.

But at long last even Jane and Katharine grew weary of merely gazing at the vain pomp and glitter, and the four children wandered on, out to the end of the pavilion, where it projected over the lake. They stood looking at the water plashing alluringly below. Presently Mark climbed over the rail and sat on the edge, and the others followed. They took off their shoes and socks and swung their legs, paddling their toes in the cool wetness (all except Martha, whose legs were too short to reach).

"How old do you suppose you have to be before you can start going to dances *really?*" said Katharine.

"*I* mean to start when I'm sixteen," said Jane.

"I think it's dumb," said Mark. "Pushing each other round an old floor, slub, slub, slub, what's the point?"

"I don't want to be sixteen, ever," said Martha. "I just want to stay the age I am."

"A lot you know!" said Jane. "Why, sixteen's the beginning of *everything!* It's just the whole crowning point of life, that's all!"

"When Mother was sixteen, she was so popular a whole lot of boys came calling at once, and they all sat in the porch swing, and there were so many they pulled the porch ceiling right *down!* She told me," said Katharine.

"*I* mean to be popular, too," said Jane, with decision. "Only we won't bother with any old porch swings. We'll drive round in sports cars."

"To fraternity house parties," said Katharine, not sure just what these were, but thinking they sounded dashing.

"And midnight canoe rides," said Jane.

"I wish we were sixteen right now, don't you?" said Katharine, trailing one foot in the water.

"Yes," said Jane, trailing one of hers, "I do."

Immediately they were.

Mark felt the change coming just before it happened,

and started to cry out, but what could he say? All he could do was watch, horrified, as his sisters' figures lengthened in the middle and their scratched legs grew slim and elegant, and their faces changed from tan and freckled to pink-and-white and powdered and uppity.

"I don't like it! Tell it to stop!" cried Martha, gazing at her expanding sisters in dismay.

"It's that magic," said Mark. "We said not every day, but nobody said anything about the nighttimes!"

Of course, if the magic had chosen to be really mean, it could have made Jane and Katharine grow up, still in their short smocked frocks and circle-combs, and they might have looked like little girls, only stretched, the way Alice did after she ate the cake that said, "Eat me."

But it took pity on their faltering youth and provided suitable dance dresses, one pink and one turquoise. And their straight un-sixteenish hair curled rapidly into a fashionable frizz, cut in the new shingle bob.

"Eek!" said the vision in pink (who seemed to be Katharine), pulling her foot quickly up out of the lake. "What nasty cold water!"

"Paddling with the little ones, how quaint," said the altered Jane.

And the two smartly-dressed flappers hurried to pull on the silken hose and satin slippers the magic had thoughtfully left in place of their cast-off socks and scuffed oxfords.

"Run along, children," said the Jane one. "Go tell your mother she wants you." And she and the Katharine one turned toward the dance floor.

Mark grabbed Martha's hand, and they hurried after them anxiously. The children's mother and Mr. Smith passed, going in the opposite direction.

"Hello, darlings, having fun?" said their mother, not noticing a thing, of course.

But two white-flanneled young men who were lounging near the dance floor seemed to notice Jane and Katharine quite a lot (which proved that they were perhaps not quite such grown-up young men as they thought they were).

One of the young men was dark, with slickum in his hair; the other sported a downy blond mustache. As Jane and Katharine drew near, the blond young man nudged his friend. The dark young man uttered a low whistle.

"I say, Topsfield," said the blond one affectedly. "What say to a spin on the floor with yon fair damsels?"

"Some keen chickens," said the dark one, smoothing his hair.

"Did you hear that?" whispered Jane to Katharine.

"Aren't they *awful?*" whispered Katharine to Jane. They giggled and preened.

"Dudes! Cake-eaters! Harold Teens!" muttered Mark furiously, in the shadows.

The young men approached. "How about a bit of the giddy whirl?" said the dark one to Jane.

"I don't mind," said Jane, tossing her head for all the world as though she really didn't.

"Shall we join the maddening throng?" said the affected blond one to Katharine.

"Charmed," said Katharine, fluttering her eyelashes.

"Ick!" Mark squirmed in his lurking-place.

"I like the dark one best, don't you? He looks like Rudolph Valentino," Martha whispered in his ear.

"He does not! He looks like a big prune!" growled Mark, savage at this desertion by his one ally.

The orchestra struck up "Three O'Clock in the Morning," and the two enchanted maidens went gliding away in the arms of their youthful cavaliers. Mark didn't know what to do next, but he thought he ought to do *something*. Some of the dance tickets Mr. Smith had bought were still in his pocket; so he grabbed Martha and shoved two tickets at the ticket taker. A second later they were sliding and hopping about the floor, pretending they were waltzing but really being detectives hot on the trail.

59

At first Mark couldn't locate either of his grown-up sisters as he tottered and heaved his way through the throng of giddy, whirling figures. At last he saw Katharine and the blond young man. They were dancing cheek-to-cheek! Katharine's eyes were closed, and the blond young man was whispering in her ear. Mark was so sickened at the sight that he forgot to lurk, and bumped straight into them.

"Really!" said the blond young man, looking down at him loftily. "What grubby children! I didn't know they allowed *babies* on the dance floor!"

"Aren't they horrid-looking? I wonder who they could be," said Katharine.

Mark stared at his sister with the open mouth of outrage.

"Shut your mouth; you'll trip and fall in it," said the blond young man, forgetting to be affected and being just a snippy sixteen-year-old.

This made Mark so angry that he squared up to the bigger boy and told him to put up his dukes. But at that moment the eddy of the dance swept Katharine and the blond young man away.

Mark looked around wildly and caught sight of the other young man with Jane. They were just leaving the dance floor. They were going to sit this one out, in the moonlight. Mark had heard of sitting dances out in the moonlight, and he was sure no good would come of it. What if the young man proposed? What if they eloped, and then Jane turned back into a little girl again, right at the altar?

Pulling Martha with him, he gave chase. Outside, Jane and the dark young man were just sitting down on a rustic bench bathed with suitable moonbeams. Mark and Martha crouched behind a handy hemlock, and peered out and listened.

"How sweet the moonlight sleeps upon this bank and all that sort of thing," said the dark young man airily, crossing his legs in a sophisticated manner.

"I adore poetry," said Jane.

The dark young man shifted nearer and made his eyes big and soulful. "The night is yet young," he said, "and romance is in the air."

"Is it?" said Jane in thrilled tones.

"Yes," said the young man, "it is. Listen. I know where I can hire this certain canoe. What say to a cruise on the rolling deep after the last dance?"

"All right," said Jane.

Mark groaned, but nobody heard him, because at that moment the band in the pavilion started playing "Home Sweet Home," and a minute later people began streaming out through the doors.

"Let's go find the others," said Jane, and she started for the pavilion, followed by the dark young man, followed by Mark and Martha. As the procession neared the entrance, the four children's mother appeared with Mr. Smith. Walking right past Jane as though she didn't see her, she came up to Martha and Mark.

"Oh, there you are," she said. "Come along, it's time for bed."

"What about Jane and Kathie?" said Martha.

"Aren't they with you? They must have gone on ahead, then. Come on."

"In a minute. I have to get something." Mark fidgeted and tried to peer past his mother.

"Have to get what?"

"Something I lost." He could see no sign anywhere now of Jane or Katharine or the young men.

Two more precious minutes were wasted in idle argument before he and Martha could escape. Once out of sight of the unwitting grownups, they ran. They ran to the pavilion. It was deserted. Then they ran down by the shore. There was a boathouse and a sign that said, "Canoes for Hire." But the man in charge was unhelpful.

"We don't hire to no kids," he said. "Gwan home." He went in and shut the door.

Mark and Martha ran to the water's edge. Over the lake

came the sound of merry voices. Someone was playing a ukulele and singing, "Paddlin' Madeline Home."

"When'll they change back, do you suppose?" said Martha anxiously. "The other magic didn't wear off till sundown; do you suppose at night it won't be till moonset? When *is* moonset?"

"I don't know," said Mark. He stood hesitant.

"Can't we unwish them?" said Martha.

"No," said Mark, "we can't. That never works. It's against the rules."

"Oh, those old rules again!" said Martha.

"Wait," said Mark. "At least we can be with them and know the worst." And hoping the time would still be ripe, he touched the lake.

Immediately they were with their sisters.

But he had forgotten to put in that they wanted to end up actually *in* the canoe; so where they found themselves was in the water, right next to it. The sudden cold plunge was quite a shock, and for a minute all Mark could do was splutter and gasp.

From the canoe (which was the extra-long tandem kind) four astonished faces gazed.

"Help! I'm drowning!" cried Martha, who nearly *was*.

The blond young man stood up and began stripping off his jacket heroically. "Be calm, ladies," he said in red-blooded tones. "Leave it all to me. I'll save her!" Then his expression changed as he recognized Mark and Martha. "Oh, it's you again," he said. "Am I going to have *more* trouble with you?"

Amazement gave way to wrath in the face of Jane. "Honestly, of all the tag-alongs!" she said. "Do you two have to follow me wherever I go?"

"Beat it, small fry!" said the dark young man rudely, strumming his ukulele.

"How perfectly mortifying!" said Katharine.

"Just a minute," said Mark. He didn't have to worry about touching the lake this time, because there was very little of him or Martha that *wasn't*. The next minute he had wished, and they were sitting drippingly in the bottom of the canoe, which was rocking dangerously.

The dark young man stopped playing his ukulele in mid-strum. "Whew!" he said admiringly. "That was some jump, kid. How'd you do it? You ought to train for aquatic sports!"

"You're dripping on my white shoes," complained the blond young man.

Mark paid them no heed. "I'm sorry," he said, "butting in like this, but I've got to tell you something. You're making a terrible mistake. I wanted to warn you before it's too late. Those girls you've got there aren't what they seem."

"They're minors," said Martha.

"Miners?" said the dark young man.

"She means minors," said Mark. He pointed at Jane. "You may not believe it, but that is a child of twelve."

"Some child!" said the dark young man, looking at Jane's willowy frame.

"They're my sisters," said Mark. "They ran away from home. I came to fetch them back. The other one's nine. They're big for their age."

"They're overgrown," added Martha helpfully.

"Of all the ridiculous stories," said Jane in disdain.

"Never in all my life!" said Katharine.

"They're sort of out of their minds right now," went on Mark, hardly knowing what he was saying. "That's why we keep them shut up."

"You'll have to think up a better story than that," said the blond young man. "I wasn't born yesterday!"

"I don't need a brick house falling down on *me!*" chimed in the dark one.

"You wouldn't like them at *all*, really," Mark rattled on desperately. "They're not your type. She bites her nails," he said, pointing at Jane, "and *she*"—he pointed at Katharine—"sucks her thumb still. Well, *sometimes* she does," he said, being fair.

"And they both play paper dolls," said Martha.

"Shame on you!" said the blond young man to Mark. "Teaching this innocent little child to tell lies that way!"

"Only a skunk would do a thing like that!" said the dark young man.

"You're right, Topsfield!" said the blond one. "You hit the nail on the head! Only a skunk!" And he glared at Mark. "She's too young to know any better, but as for you, we've had enough of your funny jokes! I give you ten seconds to get out of this canoe!"

Mark felt more desperate than ever. He didn't know what to wish, and he couldn't unwish, and at any moment the time might stop being ripe. Then he remembered what Martha had said about the magic's maybe being over when the moon set. And he touched the lake and wished quietly that it would be moonset right now.

Immediately the moon shot down the sky, fell into the lake (at least that's what it looked like), and disappeared.

"Great Scott, Topsfield!" cried the blond young man. "Did you see that comet?"

"More like a shooting star, I'd say, Wigglesworth," said the dark one. They sat blinking in the sudden darkness.

But of course you can't make a moon set just any old time. The moon was scheduled to set that morning at five-forty-one A.M., and so of course that's what it immediately was, and the dawn started coming up like gray streaks of paint above the lake, and its wan light bathed the six passengers in the canoe.

"By Jove!" said the blond young man, aghast, staring at a suddenly shrunken Katharine. "Topsfield, do you see what I see?"

"Gad, Wigglesworth!" said the dark one, looking with horror at small Jane with her nobbly knees and blue-and-white socks. "Did they look like that all along?"

"Where are we?" said Jane, like someone coming out of a trance.

"Don't you remember?" said Martha.

"I don't know," said Jane. "It's kind of mixed up."

"It's all like a dream," said Katharine.

"You're in a canoe," said Mark, beginning to enjoy himself. "These nice big boys took you for a little trip. Say thank you to the nice big boys."

"Gee. Thanks. Gosh," said Jane, in unmistakably childish and unglamorous tones. "I always wanted to ride in a canoe."

The boy called Topsfield uttered a groan. "Gad, Wigglesworth," he said. "What do you suppose came over us?"

"It must have been those lemon cokes. They must have gone to our heads," said his friend.

"Imagine!" said Topsfield. "Playing with little kids at our age! If the gang finds out about this, I'm ruined!"

"If this story gets around, my name is mud at Princeton Prep!" agreed Wigglesworth.

"We won't tell, whatever it is," Katharine assured him comfortingly. "Cross my heart and hope to die, never see the back of my neck!"

"Shall we swear it in blood?" asked Jane, producing a jackknife and holding it out in rather a grubby paw.

The boy called Topsfield winced and looked away from her.

"It's all right, old man," said Mark. "We won't any of us say a word if you just take us back to our own cottage right now."

And the big boys did, paddling fast as though they couldn't wait to see the last of them.

And though the seating accommodations were crowded and Mark and Martha were still wet to the skin, the four children enjoyed every stroke of the way, and all agreed that canoe travel was every bit as exciting as it was cracked up to be.

At last the canoe came to rest on their own familiar beach, and the four children jumped ashore.

"Mum's the word?" said the one called Topsfield anxiously.

"Silent as the tomb," Mark assured him.

"Thanks a lot, old man," said Topsfield, wringing his hand.

"That's all right, old man," said Mark, thumping him on the shoulder. And the canoe skimmed off into the morning.

As it vanished in the distance, the voice of Wigglesworth floated back over the water, still lamenting that his name would be mud at Princeton Prep.

"Aren't they silly?" said Katharine.

"Boring," Jane agreed.

"Oh, I don't know," said Mark tolerantly. "Typical sixteen-year-olds, I'd say."

"*I* think sixteen is a perfectly horrible age," said Jane. "Isn't it grim to think we'll be like that some day?"

"*I* won't," said Katharine. "I don't want to be sixteen, ever. I just want to stay the age I am."

"Well," said Mark wisely, "I guess the chances are you *will*, for a while."

And they went into the cottage.

# 4. The Storm

Of course, their mother hadn't noticed any of the magic, and never knew they hadn't come home till morning, and never said a word to Mark and Martha about their wet clothes. The clothes caused some trouble later on, though, because they shrank, and Mark and Martha had to go on wearing them for best all that year, which was sheer torture, and their mother never noticed a thing wrong.

But she noticed (and said) a good deal about the way the four children couldn't be wakened up till long past noon that day, and the way they went on being dopey and droopy and sleepy all afternoon when they *did* get up.

And since she had had a short night herself (and so had everybody else, for that matter, what with the sudden moon-setting, though of course no grownups ever knew about that), she had overslept and was tired, too, and Mr. Smith got off to work late after too little breakfast, and in general there was small time for fun and games about the cottage that day, and it wasn't till the middle of the afternoon that Mark and Jane and Katharine and Martha found themselves free and in one piece and assembled on the beach.

Mark marched straight down to the water's edge and called, "O turtle!"

"What are you going to do?" said Katharine in alarm.

"No magic! Please! Not today!" said Jane, collapsing wearily upon the sand.

Martha turned and started making tracks for the cottage.

" 'The time has come,' " Mark said, " 'to talk of many things.' "

"It won't answer. It didn't yesterday," said Jane.

"Today I think it will, somehow," said Mark.

And he was right. A few seconds later the turtle came swimming into sight. It didn't land itself on the beach, though, but stayed at a safe distance, treading water.

"Well?" it said. "Is this absolutely necessary?"

"Yes," said Mark. "Yes it is. We've got to talk things over."

"I suppose you're all pleased with yourselves about last night," said the turtle.

"Were you there? I didn't see you," said Katharine.

"I'm *always* there," said the turtle.

"No, we're not very pleased," said Mark. "I did get us home, though," he added, with a touch of justifiable pride.

"Humph," said the turtle. "Never counting the cost, of course. Just making one wish after another, hardly a minute to rest up between times, wearing a poor lake out! A lakeful of magic doesn't last forever, you know!"

"It doesn't?" said Katharine.

"Did you ever hear of anything that did?" said the turtle.

"I thought this one might," said Mark cleverly. "After all, they've never found bottom."

"Just cause they've never found it doesn't mean it isn't there," snapped the turtle. "*You*'re getting down toward the bottom already. Take that wish about being sixteen. That's a dry-land wish. Nothing watery about that. A dry-land wish takes a lot out of a lake. You've heard of a fish out of water; well, for a lake out of water it's the same principle. After this, wish wet wishes."

"We'll try," said Katharine.

"And then all that meddling with the moon," went on the turtle. "That never pays. I'd say a wish like that was worth about twenty ordinary ones. Difficult things, moons. What with the tides and all. Hard to manage. Can't say I

73

ever understood the principle of the whole thing properly myself!"

"What does it matter!" said Jane. "When the magic gets really shallow we can just wish on you, and fill it up again."

"No," said the turtle, "that's just what you *can't* do. Not any more. It's out of my hands now. The lake's stronger than I am."

"It is?" said Martha, who had edged back to join the group.

"It is, since you made that first wish," said the turtle. "It's hard to explain. You mere babes and sucklings wouldn't understand."

"Why, you!" said Martha, who was sensitive about being called a baby.

"I think I kind of see," said Mark. "You had the power to make the lake full of magic, but now it's bigger than you are. Like Frankenstein."

"Exactly," said the turtle, "and you know what happened to *him!* I suggest after this you think twice before you wish anything at all."

"We're going to," said Mark. "That's why I called you. We want to be safe and sane from now on. And I think we need one more rule. No magic except every third day. Then we'll know when to expect what."

"When I gave you those three extra wishes," said the turtle, "you promised that would be absolutely all."

"We didn't know then what we know now," said Mark.

The turtle looked thoughtful. Then it shook its head. "I couldn't take the chance," it said. "With that lake in the mood it's in now, dear me knows what it might do. That's a tired lake."

"All right, then," said Mark. With a sudden pounce he splashed into the water and caught hold of the turtle with both hands.

"Bully!" said the turtle, struggling in his grasp. "Brute force never solved anything yet."

"Sure," said Mark. "Naturally. I wouldn't try a thing like that. I just want to talk a little more."

He knelt down till his face was on a level with the turtle's and looked it in the eye. "You know," he said, "Kathie was saying just the other day that we ought to have some way of knowing you when we see you, so you won't seem just like any old Tom, Dick, or Harry of a turtle. It'd be more friendly. And I was thinking. I saw a turtle once, in a shopwindow, that was keen. All painted white it was, with pink rosebuds."

"No!" cried the turtle in heart-rending tones. "You wouldn't do that. You couldn't. I'd be branded for life as a mere household pet, a domestic slave! It would be the end of me socially! Say you won't do it, and I'll grant any wish you like!"

"Just the one I said," said Mark.

"Unloose me," said the turtle. Mark did. The turtle assumed an expression of great concentration. Then it relaxed. "That's done it," it said. "The lake put up a fight, but I pushed it through."

"Every third day?" said Mark.

"Every third day," said the turtle.

"Counting from today?"

"Counting from today."

"Thanks," said Mark.

"Don't mention it," said the turtle with dignity. "And now may I go?"

Mark's conscience smote him. "No hard feelings?" he asked.

The turtle looked at him. "Oh, no," it said. "Certainly not. I *love* having great two-footed creatures invading my privacy and wearing out my lake and interfering with my way of life. I *adore* catering to their silly wishes. It's my one hobby!" But Mark thought it winked at him as it swam away.

He stood up. "So now," he said, "we know where we stand."

"Yes," said Jane. "I guess we've got everything just about under control now."

76

"And we can relax and forget about the magic for two whole days!" said Martha.

"As though we *could!*" said Katharine.

But it was surprising how nearly they did. That first day was just about over already, and they were only too willing to drag their exhausted selves to bed right after supper. That night of the early moonset had taken a lot out of *them*, as well as the lake.

The next day, when Mr. Smith had left for work, their mother asked them if they thought it would be fun to take a picnic lunch and go for a trip in the excursion launch called the *Willa Mae.* So they did, and soon all was white-caps and brass railings and blue distances and people waving from the shore.

As they were eating their lunch (hard-boiled eggs and spring-onion-and-radish sandwiches), Jane turned to Mark.

"If this were one of the magic days," she said, "we could be rounding the Horn."

"The mighty schooner strained at its seams, and the sails sang in the hurricane," agreed Katharine.

"Or we could be explorers charting unknown seas," said Mark.

"*There*'s a good unknown sea now," said Martha, as the *Willa Mae* passed an inlet all choked with waterweeds, and a broken-down cottage beside it that looked haunted, at *least.*

But pretty soon they stopped at an amusement park on the far side of the lake and stayed there for two whole hours, and the thought of magic was thrown to the winds as all donned bathing suits and slid down shoot-the-chutes that came to a watery end amid splashes and the ear-splitting screams of utter enjoyment.

That night just before bedtime the four children met in solemn council.

"Don't anyone dare *think* a wish between now and after breakfast," said Jane.

"That's going to be hard," said Mark. "Like remembering to say 'Rabbit, rabbit,' when you wake up on the first of the month."

"Everybody think wet thoughts all night, just in case somebody forgets," said Katharine. "We want to pamper that lake."

"I bet I wake up first," said Martha.

"If you do, let's not have any going down to the lake ahead of the rest of us," said Mark. "The first one up wakes the others, and we plan." And all agreed.

As it turned out, it was Katharine who opened her eyes first the next morning.

It was a flash of lightning that made her open them.

And then came a gigantic crash of thunder that woke the others, and after that the rain came pelting and blowing all o. .r the screened porch, and the four children made a mad dash for indoors.

Too late they remembered about the magic and started to dash out again, but their mother was up by now and barred the way.

"Nobody goes near that lake this morning," she said. "Water's dangerous in a thunderstorm."

"But we *have* to!" said Jane. "Just for a minute!"

"It won't hurt us. It *knows* us," said Martha. "It's *expecting* us!"

"Stop talking nonsense and help get breakfast," said their mother.

"It's probably only a shower, anyway," said Mark. "We can wait."

But it wasn't. It kept on raining and raining for what seemed like hours. And even though the thunder and lightning were fewer and farther between now, their mother was still firm.

"Wouldn't you know?" said Jane. "Now everything's just utterly and completely ruined!"

"I think it's trying to clear up," said Katharine, at a window.

For answer there came a really blinding flash that drove her back into the middle of the room, and the rain redoubled its force on the roof.

79

"Hark!" said their mother, coming into the room from saying good-by to Mr. Smith. "What's that?"

*That* was a dripping sound and proved to come from a leak in the roof, in a corner just over one of the indoor cots. While their mother ran to get something to put under it, Mark discovered another leak in the kitchen ceiling, and Jane found one merrily plip-plopping right in the middle of the upstairs bedroom.

Five minutes later the fourth leak was discovered, and they were beginning to run out of dishpans and double-boiler-bottoms. The sound of water dripping tinnily into pots made an interesting obbligato to the music of the storm.

The four children sat around the dishpan on the living-room floor (the cot had been moved out of the way for the sake of the sheets) and watched the water gradually filling it. Carrie the cat, who didn't like thunderstorms, came and sat next to them, and Martha absent-mindedly took her in her lap.

"How many drops make a gallon?" said Katharine, not because she really wanted to know, but because there was nothing better to say. Nobody knew the answer.

"Where does it all *come* from?" said Martha, a prey to exasperation.

It was then that the sudden brilliant thought struck the

mind of Jane. "Why, it comes from the lake!" she cried. "Doesn't it? Sure it does! It's scientific! The sun draws the water up, and then it condenses and comes down again, and that's rain! This is lake water we've got right here in this pan!"

"Will it be magic still, after it's been through all that?" said Katharine.

"Why not? Condensed magic!"

"It ought to be even stronger, if it's anything like condensed milk!"

"At least we can try!"

The four children hung over the dishpan, all talking at once.

"What in the world are you doing?" said their mother, passing through the room. "You look like witches round a caldron." She went out again.

"Do you suppose she's begun to notice?" whispered Martha.

"Probably just a quincidence," said Mark. "Now. Everybody keep calm. Let's plan. Take it slowly. Start big and narrow down. Do we want to go somewhere in time, or just space? Or both?"

"I never can think what anything means when you put it like that," said Martha. "It sounds too much like schoolwork."

"We have to keep it wet," said Katharine, who was often of a one-track mind. "What wet things are fun?"

"Niagara Falls in a barrel? Battle of Trafalgar? Ulysses?" said Jane, reading from one of her many lists.

"No," said everybody else.

"Start the other way round," said Mark. "What fun things are wet?"

"Sailboating," said Jane promptly.

"Too real," objected Katharine.

An idea dawned in Mark. "What do you say?" he said, and broke off. His eyes took on a glazed expression.

"To what?" said Martha.

"No," muttered Mark. "That wouldn't work."

"*What* wouldn't?" said Katharine.

"On the other hand, though," said Mark, and stopped again.

"Do you want us to scream?" said Jane.

"Well," said Mark, "I was just thinking. What's snow, if it isn't water sort of frozen? And who's ever had *really* enough snow at one time? And where is there the most of it to be had?"

"The North Pole!" said Jane.

"We could see Santa Claus," said Martha. The others were too considerate of her tender youth to comment on this.

"No," said Mark. "Not the North, that's too tame. But the South one hasn't been discovered yet, hardly."

"We could find it and claim it for the United States of America," said Katharine, her eyes shining with the spirit of true patriotism.

"What do you say?" said Mark. "Shall we wish?"

"It's certainly wet enough," said Jane.

"Put in about having warm clothes," said Katharine.

"And not catching cold," said Martha.

"We could take along hot possets," said Jane.

There was a pause, while cocoa was hastily brewed. A few moments later, clutching the steaming mugs of it, the four children clustered round the dishpan again.

"Let's all touch at once," said Katharine. "That'll be more sort of mystic."

The hands that weren't clutching the cocoa went out toward the dishpan.

"Look!" said Jane, pointing at the water. Already a thin scum of ice was forming across its top. "It thinks it's a good idea. It *wants* us to!"

The next minute all hands had touched and all hearts had wished.

And the minute after *that*, the dishpan had disappeared, and the water in it had turned white and frozen and grown bigger and bigger until it was a vast snowy plain, and the four children found themselves seated in the middle of it, suitably bundled up and befurred, and with mugs of cocoa still in their now fur-mittened hands.

Carrie the cat found herself there, too, through no wish of her own, for Martha had forgotten to put her off her lap.

"Brr!" said everybody, in the sudden wintry blast, and four noses were buried in four steaming mugs.

"Whiff!" said Carrie, putting back her whiskers. She took one or two delicate steps across the snowy crust, not sure whether she liked it.

Thawed by cocoa, the four children stood up and peered around interestedly.

"Is this all there is to it?" said Martha, looking at snowy whiteness and nothing else as far as the eye could see.

"What did you expect?" said Mark. "A big post sticking up?"

"I just thought there might be more *to* it, somehow," said Martha.

Still, if the magic said this was the South Pole, this must be it. So Mark, who always had pencils, took one out, and using the eraser end, wrote an inscription in the snow.

"South Pole. Prop. of U.S.A. We found it."

After that he put the date, and they all signed their

84

names. Martha had Carrie sign her paw-print, too. Carrie did not seem to appreciate the privilege. And that seemed to be that.

But *after* that there were snowballs to be thrown, and a snowman to be built, and ice to be found and slid on, and if you have ever been transported suddenly from a hot and thundery day in July to the middle of a Winter Sports Carnival in December, you will have some idea of how the next fleeting moments happily passed.

"Darn!" said Jane. "We should have put in a toboggan while we were wishing!"

"And skis!" said Katharine.

"And snowshoes!" said Mark.

"Who cares?" said Martha. "Let's lie down and make angels." And she and Katharine did.

It was just as the four children were organizing a game of fox-and-geese (and wishing they'd brought more people along so there'd be enough to play it properly) that the cry was heard in the distance.

"What was that?" said Jane. "It sounded human."

"Eskimos!" said Martha.

"They don't have those *here*," said Katharine. "That's Alaska."

"What *do* they have, then?"

"They don't. It's uninhabited," said Mark.

"So far as anyone *knows*," said Jane.

Martha's lip trembled. "I don't *like* things that live where it's uninhabited!"

Just then the cry was heard again, and nearer now, and as the four children looked around to see where it had come from, a furred and booted figure staggered into view. It seemed to see them, and started forward in a kind of tottering rush, and as it drew nearer, they could see that it was a man. But they couldn't tell much else about him, because his face was covered with about a week's growth of beard. The sight was not a reassuring one, and Martha turned to flee.

But the man seemed just as upset by them as they were by him. As he came nearer, he stopped short, rubbed his eyes, gave a despairing moan, sank on his knees in the snow, and covered his face with his hands.

"It's all over. Might as well give up now," he cried in something between a sob and a shudder. "Now I'm seeing things! Angel children dancing in a ring!" He peered between his fingers. "Now they're gone. It's the beginning of the end. My mind's given way. Might as well lie down and die right here!"

"No, don't do that," said Katharine, ever sympathetic, edging forward to see if she could be of some help.

"We're not angels," said Mark.

86

"We're not even specially good," said Jane.

"We're just children," said Martha.

The man groaned and covered his ears. "Now I'm hearing voices!" he said. "I hope the end comes quickly. I can't stand any more!"

"It's no use," said Mark. "It's that thing of grownups noticing a little, but not much. He thinks we're spooks."

The four children stood looking at the man. And now an expression of even greater horror came over his face, and he gave a terrible cry. He was staring at something beyond them, and they turned and followed his gaze.

Carrie the cat stepped forward, picking her way elegantly along and waving her tail. And maybe because she hadn't really been part of the wish but had only got into it more or less by accident, the man seemed to see her all too clearly.

"No!" he cried, waving her away and shutting his eyes to blot out the sight. "No! Scat, you horrid beast! Now I *know* I'm really crazy! If it were a polar bear now, I might believe it. Or a Saint Bernard dog with a bottle of brandy round its neck!"

"Poor thing. I wish we had some brandy, don't you?" said Katharine.

"There's the cocoa," said Jane.

And now a strange thing happened. The four children

could never decide afterwards whether Carrie did it deliberately or not. Certainly she had never gone out of her way to be helpful to anyone before. But now she walked majestically over to where the four mugs of cocoa still stood, balanced on the snowy crust where the four children had put them down. She leaned delicately over one of the mugs. There was a sound of lapping.

The man had followed her, as though hypnotized, and though he didn't see the cocoa (for hot possets had been part of the wish), he heard the lapping. And throwing table manners to the winds, he flung himself down on the snow and sought its source with his mouth. The four children looked away politely.

And now the man began to laugh hysterically. "Ha ha ha!" he cried. "Cocoa! If it weren't so tragic, it'd be funny. I said I'd find the South Pole or die, but I thought it would be a hero's death. I never thought I'd spend my last hours drinking cocoa with a domestic cat!" But he drank the cocoa.

And even though it was invisible to him, it seemed to do him good. For he perked up noticeably, and the flush of health began to appear on his wan cheek (such of it as could be seen between whiskers).

"Now I know what he's doing here," said Mark. "He's an explorer and he's lost. He's trying to find the South Pole."

"Oh, is that all? Why doesn't he look, then?" said Martha. "It's right behind him."

"He doesn't notice it," said Katharine. "He doesn't see our inscription, either. It's invisible to him."

"We could help," said Jane. "We could sort of shove him along with our ghostly unseen hands till he's right on it."

"No we couldn't," said Mark. "Then he really *would* go mad. No mortal mind could stand it."

And it turned out not to be necessary. For now, having drained her half of the mug of cocoa, Carrie started parading slowly toward the inscription Mark had written in the snow. Every few steps she turned and looked over her shoulder at the man. Fascinated, he followed her.

Carrie reached the spot, sat down on it, and purred. The man came and stood beside her. Suddenly an idea dawned. He took out his compass. He took his bearings. And a great light broke over his face.

"Eureka!" he cried. "At last, at last! After all these years! Oh, what a lucky fellow I am!" He took out a whistle and blew it. He started shouting and waving his arms.

"Admiral!" he called. "Fellows! Barriscale, Chelmsford, McAlpine! Here it is! I found it! We've done it! We're successful, we're famous, we're heroes!"

And from the distance four more figures came stagger-

ing into view, furred and booted and bearded and pale and tottering, but with excited grins and joyful flushes marking each face. They ran up to the first man. *They* took out their compasses. *They* took their bearings. And then they all began jumping for joy and thumping each other on the back in congratulation and dancing round and round the Pole in delight.

"How did you ever find this spot in the first place, Fordyce?" said one of the men to the first man.

"I don't know. Something just seemed to lead me to it," said Fordyce. "Instinct, I guess."

"Isn't he going to give even *Carrie* any credit?" said Katharine to Mark.

Carrie was wreathing herself around the men's legs now and making conversation.

"What's that sound?" said the fourth man. "Kind of a meowing and wawling."

"For a minute I thought I saw a pussycat," said another.

"But that couldn't be, of course," said still another. "Not in the Antarctic."

"We don't want to go home saying we saw a thing like that," said the one who seemed to be the Admiral. "Nobody would believe a thing we *do* say. Nobody would believe we found the Pole at all."

All of the men were looking straight at Carrie now.

"I don't see a thing, do you, fellows?" said Fordyce.

"Not a thing," said all the others.

"Come on," said the one called the Admiral. "Let's get back to the plane and broadcast the good news home to the States."

And still clapping each other on the back and rejoicing in their good fortune, they hurried off across the snow.

"Wait!" called Martha after them. The others didn't even bother.

"Really!" said Jane. "Some people!"

"And now I suppose we just go home," said Katharine.

"No, we don't," said Mark. "Not till sundown. Remember?"

Everybody looked at the sun. It shone brightly, straight above them. Time passed. They looked at it again. It hadn't moved an inch and didn't look as if it intended to. And then Mark remembered something.

"Oh-oh," he said. "We're at the South Pole, remember? Didn't you ever hear of the midnight sun? When there *is* any sun at all down here, it hardly *ever* sets. Sometimes not for weeks, I guess."

"And here we are," said Katharine.

"And here we'll be," said Jane.

"I want Mother," said Martha.

After that nobody said anything for a few minutes. "Who wants to throw snowballs?" said Mark finally.

Nobody did.

"Now I know where the snows of yesteryear are," said Katharine. "They're all here. They must be."

"Now I see why people go to Florida in the winter," said Jane. "I for one will never build a snowman again."

Mark cleared his throat. "O turtle?" he said.

"Don't be silly," said Jane. "It couldn't come here. It'd freeze."

"*We*'re here and *we*'re not freezing, are we?" said Mark.

"*Who* isn't?" said Martha bitterly.

At that moment a voice spoke at their elbow. "Hello," it said.

The four children turned. An odd figure in nunlike black-and-white confronted them.

"You're a penguin," said Katharine.

"Naturally," said the penguin.

Carrie the cat arched her back and hissed. She could not abide a bird.

"Do you know our turtle? Did it send you to help us? Are penguins magic, too?" said Martha.

"Don't we look as though we were?" said the penguin. And the four children had to admit that this was true.

"Wish us home, then," said Martha.

"Make the sun set," said Katharine.

"Please," said Mark, either because he had better manners than the others or because he was more tactful.

"It's not so simple as that," said the penguin.

"Naturally. It never is," said Jane.

"As you ought to know by now," agreed the penguin. "However. Just sit there patiently for a bit. Perhaps I'll think of something."

The four children sat there patiently while the penguin paced up and down, deep in thought. Carrie the cat followed the penguin with her eyes. She crouched low to the ground, her tail lashing. She started forward.

"Call off this fierce marauding beast," said the penguin. "I can't think when I'm being stalked."

Martha took Carrie in her lap.

"That's better," said the penguin. "Now then. Follow me. I have a plan."

It led the way, and the four children followed, Martha still keeping tight hold of Carrie. Carrie's lip curled in disgust every time she looked at the penguin. Presently they came in sight of an endless-looking wind-swept sea, with a great mass of ice at its edge.

"That's probably the Antarctic Ocean," said Mark, who knew about such things. "That's probably a glacier just up ahead."

Even as he spoke, there was a crash, and a sizable mass of ice detached itself from the shore and went floating away over the cold, vasty deep.

94

"Hop on," said the penguin. "The next iceberg leaves in two minutes."

The four children hopped where it pointed and sat down on cold slipperiness that moved. A few seconds later there was another crash, and a crack appeared between them and the penguin. The crack widened rapidly into a watery gulf, and the four children found themselves sailing away in the wake of the previous iceberg.

"Good-by!" they called, waving at the shore. "Thanks a lot!" The penguin flipped a flipper. Carrie uttered a parting snarl.

And then shore and penguin were lost to view, and there was nothing to be seen on either hand but cold water and other bobbing icebergs.

"Hard-a-lee!" said Jane. "This is as good as being on a yacht. Well, almost."

"My sitting-down part's cold," said Martha. "It's damp, too."

"Do icebergs always go this fast?" said Katharine. "We're passing all those others already. And I think it's getting warmer."

"Isn't it?" said Jane. "That penguin must have sent us by special express. We must be getting up in the Temperate Zone already."

"*I* think we're shrinking," said Martha. "Look!"

Jane and Katharine looked. It was true. The edges of their icy float were visibly melting away before their eyes.

"This is awful," said Jane. "We're down to half-size already. How long do you suppose we'll last?"

Mark said nothing. He was scanning the horizon. Now he suddenly took off his coat and started waving it. "Ship ahoy!" he called.

A ship had appeared on the horizon and was steaming swiftly toward them. Soon it was so near that the four children could see the faces of the people who lined the deck. But the faces didn't seem friendly a bit.

"Keep away!" called the people on the ship. "How dare you run your nasty old iceberg across our course? Don't come any nearer. You'll run us down!"

And the ship turned in craven flight and hurried away, fearful of being rammed and caved in. "Though for all the damage we could do by now," said Jane, "we might as well be a mere popsicle!"

It was true. The iceberg had dwindled away till there was barely room for the four of them and Carrie to sit, huddled together as closely as they could huddle. The four children took off the thick coats the magic had provided in order to make more room (and because it was growing so very hot all of a sudden), and the coats sank to a watery grave as the edges of the iceberg melted away under them.

"Darn!" said Katharine. "I liked mine lots better than my regular winter one."

"Never mind," said Jane. "They'd probably have vanished at sundown, anyway."

"Speaking of sun," said Mark, dashing perspiration from his forehead and beginning to take off his shirt, "this must be the tropics. It's hot!"

"The tropics?" cried Martha in alarm. "You know what they have there, don't you? Sharks!"

Katharine glanced ahead. She turned pale. "Don't look!" she cried; so of course everyone did.

A curved fin was bearing down toward them. No one needed to be told whose fin it was. Martha began to cry.

"Don't give up. Not yet," said Mark grimly. "Look over there."

Everybody looked the other way. The tropical sun, a hot red ball, was sinking toward the blue waves. In its heat the last remnants of the iceberg were dissolving fast. The four children could hear small tinkles and crackings below them now as its underpinnings gave way, and when they looked down, they could see heaving sea through the poor final fragment that was just big enough to bear their weight. It was a race between the iceberg and the sun. The shark could afford to wait. Martha had her hands over her eyes, but she peeked between her fingers and saw the curved fin hovering nearby.

Then the last thin ice melted, and the four children felt themselves sinking. But they didn't plunge into watery saltness, or into sharky, toothy sharpness either. For as the iceberg sank, so did the sun, and the four children landed with a thud on hard, dry flooring.

They were sitting in a circle on the living-room floor looking at a dishpan full of water.

Their mother came into the room. "What are you doing in here?" she said. "The storm stopped ages ago. Don't you want to go swimming?"

Mark and Martha and Jane and Katharine rose crampedly to their feet and staggered to fetch their bathing suits. And the mind of each grappled dazedly with the fact that it was still only morning after the long full day they'd already had.

As they came out into the sunlight, a black-and-white towhee was scratching among the weeds near the porch. Thinking it was the penguin grown to handier, convenient size, Carrie hurried away after it.

The four children paid her no heed. The lake was waiting. They ran into it.

# 5. The Bottle

When Mr. Smith came home from the bookshop that evening, he brought newspapers with him, and the newspapers had staring headlines. Some American explorers had discovered the South Pole.

"Isn't it exciting?" said the children's mother.

"Oh, that," said Martha.

"It's all right, I guess," said Jane, "if you like that kind of thing."

But as soon as they were alone, the four children read the newspaper accounts through carefully. None of the stories made any mention of Carrie, and they didn't say anything about four ghostly children, either.

"It's not fair," said Jane. "It was our best chance of going down in history, so far. Now I'll have to think of something else."

"I don't mind for myself," said Martha. "It's Carrie. You'd think the least they could do would be name the continent after her!"

"Little Cattia," said Mark.

"Feline Island," said Katharine.

"New Carrie," said Jane.

There was a pause. "Oh, well," said Mark. "At least we'll always know we were a part of it."

"We can feel secretly proud," said Katharine.

"Virtue is its own reward," said Martha.

"It would be," said Jane. "As if it weren't dull enough already! It's adding insult to injury." But she cut the newspaper stories out and put them away in her top bureau drawer just the same.

The reason the four children were alone was that their mother and Mr. Smith were in the upstairs bedroom talking. They talked for a long time, and dinner was late, and after dinner (and dishes) their mother and Mr. Smith kept looking at each other as if they had something on their minds and wanted to be alone with it, and kept asking the four children if they weren't tired and didn't want to go to bed early, until at last the four children saw the point and decided to humor the poor hapless adults, and they *went* to bed. And Jane and Katharine and Martha went to sleep.

Mark went to sleep for a while, but then he woke up. The reason he woke up was that their mother and Mr. Smith had come downstairs from their bedroom for a midnight snack and were sitting in the living room having it. And the light shone in Mark's eyes on the sleeping porch, and he could hear every word they said.

Of course, he knew perfectly well that eavesdropping is wrong, and he probably should have called out and warned them, but by the time he thought of this he'd already heard so much he decided it would be embarrassing. And besides, he wasn't dropping from the eaves; he was lying obediently in his own bed, and if people *would* come talking right by an open window right next to him, he couldn't help that, could he? And besides, it was interesting.

So he lay low and said nothing. After a while their mother and Mr. Smith put out the living-room light and went upstairs. But still Mark lay awake for a long time thinking.

Right after breakfast next morning, before swimming or anything, he called a conference. And because the sight of the lake might prove too tantalizing, when there was nothing they could do about it till day after tomorrow, he called it on the other side of the cottage, the side next to the pasture with the sheep and the unfriendly rams. Jane and Katharine and Martha sat in a row on the split-rail fence and listened, while Mark perched on a boulder and drew patterns in the earth with a stick, as he talked.

"The thing is," he said, "this summer may be all very well for us, and a consolation devoutly to be wished, but it's hard on Mr. Smith," (for he could never bring himself to say Uncle Huge, the way Martha did). "He has to run all this and the bookshop, too. He's having to kind of lead a double life."

"Like Dr. Jekyll and Mr. Hyde," said Katharine.

"Only different," said Jane.

"And the thing is," said Mark, "it's beginning to Tell on him. His Business is Suffering. And he's worried about it. I heard him tell Mother so."

"He looks tired, too," said Martha. "All that driving back and forth."

"And it's all our fault," said Katharine. "We've been enjoying the magic, and wasting its sweetness on our own desert air, and never thinking of others at all."

"We've got to do something," said Jane.

"What'll we do?" said Martha.

"That's the whole point," said Mark. "The next wish has got to be for *him*."

"You're right," said Jane. "It's only fair."

"What'll we wish?" said Martha.

"That's the whole point," said Mark again. "We don't want to rush off half-cocked, the way we did when we tried to help Mother with the half-magic that other time. Remember what happened."

They remembered.

"No," he went on, "this time we've really got to think it over first. And that's why it's good that we've got two whole days before the magic. We can be thinking."

"Good," said Jane. "We'll do that."

"Let's," said Katharine.

Martha nodded her head earnestly.

And with that settled, the four children forgot all about Mr. Smith for the moment and turned their minds happily to the important question of how they were to while away the golden hours in the meantime.

It was a blue-skied morning, and the sun shone brightly but coolly, and a fresh wind blew.

"This," said Mark, "is the kind of day when the open road calls."

"Let's explore," said Jane.

"We already did," said Martha.

"Not that old South Pole," said Jane in tones of scorn. "Let's explore our own territory. See America first. We've never found out where that red-clay road *goes*."

"We could take our lunch," said Katharine.

"What kind of sandwiches?" said Mark.

"Jam," said Martha thoughtfully, "and peanut-butter-and-banana, and cream-cheese-and-honey, and date-and-nut, and prune-and-marshmallow . . ."

A time passed.

Their mother came into the kitchen. "What's all this mess?" she said. "Nobody leaves this house till it's cleaned up."

And nobody did.

By the time Jane and Mark and Katharine were ready to go, the sun had climbed lots higher in the sky and wasn't half so cool. And they had made so many sandwiches and tasted the important parts of each so many times to get just the right blends that by now everybody's gorge rose and nobody felt like having a picnic for ages, at least. But they packed the lunch basket with the sandwiches, anyway.

"Where's Martha?" asked somebody.

It turned out nobody had seen her for some time.

"Here I am," said a voice at that moment. "Are we all ready?" And a small figure walked in from outside.

"No thanks to you," said Mark. "Workshirk."

"I had something to do," said Martha.

"Naturally," said Jane. "At a time like this. Just for that you get to carry the lunch basket." And Martha did.

The four children went over the rolling meadow with

the sheep, keeping well out of the way of the un-
trustworthy rams, and came into the red-clay road some
distance beyond the farm where the milk came from.
From now on all was unexplored territory, and they explored it.

Once some bluebirds flew over saying, "Tru-a-lee," and
for a while there were some bright yellow wild flowers
growing by the side of the road that Mark, who always
knew about such things, said were tansy, also called bitter
buttons. Jane, ever venturesome, tasted a few and said they
were bitter all right. None of the others cared to try.

But otherwise, one red-clay hill proved very much like
another, and they kept going on and on, and there didn't
seem to be any end to them, until at the top of the third one
Martha, who hadn't been in on all the sandwich-making
and who had been carrying the heavy basket all this while,
sat down by the side of the road and said she wasn't going a step farther until she had her lunch right here and
now.

"Not out here in the sun like this," said Katharine, wip-
ing perspiration from her eyebrows. "Human flesh couldn't
stand it. It'd broil."

"There's a woods coming," said Mark, pointing ahead.
"If we just keep on, we're sure to find an ideal spot."

So he and Jane and Katharine and a reluctant Martha

trudged down the third hill and toiled up the fourth, and at the top of it the woods came right up to the side of the road, and there proved to be a track that turned off and went in among the trees, and the four children followed it.

"Coolth," said Katharine. "Blessed, blessed coolth."

"That's no word," said Jane.

"It ought to be," said Katharine, pressing on.

A woods in August isn't quite the magic thing that it is in early spring, when birds are still fresh-voiced and violets are pushing through. Still, a woods is a woods, and the four children hadn't been in one for weeks at least, and there were branches to swing from (Mark), and side paths to explore (Jane), and ferns to collect and keep dropping (Katharine), and all the time Martha kept finding one ideal spot after another, and the other three kept saying they weren't quite ideal enough.

At last they came to a clearing with a brook curving through, and though it wasn't the babbling time of the year, there was still a satisfactorily wet trickling at the bottom, and Jane sat down on the bank and took off her shoes and socks and put her feet in the water and announced that this was the place for her. So then there were the sandwiches to be unpacked and divided with scrupulous fairness, and after that Jane traded all her peanut-butter-and-banana for all Katharine's prune-and-marshmallow, and after that nobody said anything for a long time.

"Now," said Martha finally. "What are we going to do about Uncle Huge and the magic?"

"We can't do anything," said Mark. "Not yet."

"What are we going to do when we *do* do something?" said Martha, sounding like a popular song, as Katharine pointed out.

A discussion of the chief ballads of the day followed, and a stirring rendition of "Do, Do, Do What You've Done, Done, Done Before" on the part of Jane and Katharine. When silence had been restored, Martha returned to the subject.

"I've been thinking," she said, "about that treasure."

"What treasure?" said Katharine.

"The treasure on the island, silly," said Mark. "The pirate treasure, the treasure in the chest. I've been thinking about it, too."

"Why, yes!" Jane joined in excitedly. "Sure! That pirate captain marked the stone with his initials as plain as plain! We could find it and dig it up in no time! It's a cinch!"

"Of course, we never saw inside it," said Katharine, "but you can guess what it'd be. Would pieces of eight still be worth anything after all these years?"

"Rare coin collectors would give untold millions," said

Mark. "There're probably jewels there, too. We could probably give Mother some and still have enough left over to put us all on Easy Street!"

"That's what we'll do, then," said Jane.

"I thought of it first," said Martha.

"Day after tomorrow," said Katharine. "I can't wait."

"We'll get back to the house now and plan," said Mark.

To pack the empty sandwich papers in the lunchbox and bury the unsightly crusts (of which there were a good many) was but the work of a moment, and the four children set upon the homeward trek.

"Which direction?" Katharine wondered.

"That-a-way," said Mark, pointing, and then starting through the trees. Everyone else followed.

Ten minutes later they were still walking, and there was still no sign of the red-clay road.

"It ought to be right ahead any minute now," said Mark.

But it wasn't. What *was* right ahead was a clearing, with a brook curving through and a stray sandwich paper somebody had forgotten caught in a bush and rustling in the breeze.

"We've come in a circle," said Jane.

"Are we lost?" said Martha, beginning to sound scared.

"Pooh," said Mark. "That's nothing. That always happens in a woods. You veer toward the left cause your heart's on that side."

"Well," said Jane, "it's nice to know our hearts are on the right side, anyway."

"Left," Mark corrected her.

"You know what I mean," said Jane.

"Maybe if we all sort of leaned toward the right and tried again," said Katharine.

This didn't sound very sensible and looked even sillier, but the four children were willing to try anything. Turning their backs to the brook, they walked lopsidedly away. A time passed.

"I've seen that stick before," said Katharine, pointing at the ground.

"That's not a stick, it's a branch," said Jane.

"Whatever it is," said Katharine. "I remember that knobbly part. We're in a circle again."

A few steps farther on, the familiar brook appeared.

"We *are* lost," said Martha, sounding really scared now. The four children sat down on the bank and faced this fact.

"Now I know what it means about not seeing the woods for the trees," said Jane, looking round at the curtain of green.

"I for one," said Katharine, "will never feel the same about Arbor Day again."

"If that brook were the lake," said Jane, "we could touch it and wish ourselves home right now."

"And if it were day after tomorrow," Mark reminded her.

"Oh, those old rules!" said Martha. "Always making things harder!"

"We asked for them, don't forget," said Mark. "It was worse when we didn't have any."

"Maybe we should call the turtle," said Katharine. "It sent a penguin before."

"What would it send in a woods?" Jane wondered. "A moose, maybe."

"O turtle?" said Mark, but not as if he expected any answer.

Still, everybody looked round in every direction, just the same. Nothing passed by but a caterpillar who was just looking.

"It can't come," said Mark. "The magic's bigger than it is now. It said so."

"Yes, it did, didn't it?" said Martha in rather a peculiar voice. "Then if we had some lake water here now, we could *make* it come, couldn't we?"

"If," said Mark. "If!"

"Well?" said Martha. And she triumphantly drew a small bottle from her pocket.

"That's Mother's best French perfume," said Jane.

"It *was*," said Martha. "She used the last drop the night

we all went to the dance. She said I could have the bottle for my handkerchief drawer. It's got lake water in it right now. I went down to the beach and got some before we started, just in case!"

She finished and looked round at the others proudly and defiantly, and everybody's heart sank. Because everybody knew Martha had got over being scared now and was going to be awful. That was always the way with Martha, and when she was that way, there was no doing anything with her.

"This is terrible," Katharine wailed. "She'll make the turtle come, and that'll break all the rules, and the magic'll be out of control again! Wait!" she begged Martha. "Remember how it was that first day! Remember that big snake thing?"

"Give me that bottle," said Jane, "before you do something foolish."

"I won't," said Martha. "What do I care about those old rules, or that old snake thing either? If we wait till day after tomorrow, Uncle Huge could go bankrupt in the meantime! We've got to get him that treasure right now!"

"Careful," said Mark. "Every time we ever broke rules before it brought us nothing but disaster!"

"I don't care," said Martha. "Anyway, I'm tired of woods and my feet hurt."

"Of course *that*'s the whole point," said Jane. "Shame on you! Pretending you're doing it for Mr. Smith when all along you're just being selfish!"

"Oh, I am, am I?" cried Martha in a rage. "Just for that I'll do the whole thing by myself, and you needn't any of you even bother to come along! You can stay here and wait for three days for all I care! I don't need you and I don't need that old turtle, either!" And pulling the stopper from the bottle, she dashed its contents recklessly all over her hands and front. "I wish," she cried, "that all the rules were broken and I was on that island with the pirate's treasure this minute!"

And she was.

It all happened so quickly that not even Mark could do a thing to stop her. All he and Jane and Katharine could do was stand staring stupidly at the spot where Martha had been and where she now suddenly wasn't any more. And if you have ever looked at a spot where somebody suddenly isn't any more, you will have some idea of how he and Jane and Katharine felt.

A chill wind sprang up and blew through the empty space, just to make it eerier.

Some drops of water that had rolled off Martha's hands splashed to the ground.

"Quick!" cried Katharine. "Touch them and wish!"

But the drops of water didn't behave like ordinary drops of water at all. They didn't form a pool, or soak into the ground, but gathered themselves together and went rolling along like bits of mercury when you let the thermometer fall and break it (as you always do). And before anybody could touch any of the little rolling balls, they had bounced down the bank and joined the mossy trickle of the brook.

"Now it's all diluted!" cried Jane.

"Touch it anyway!" cried Katharine.

Mark threw himself down by the edge of the brook, stuck his finger in, and wished with all his might.

Nothing happened.

"I guess the magic's gone out of it," he said.

"Either that," said Jane, "or it's watered down below human strength."

"What'll we do?" said Katharine. "We've got to get out of this woods somehow and save her from herself!"

"If we only had a compass," said Jane.

"Wait," said Mark. "I've been watching the sun. Back there before any of this started happening. It's been going *that* way." He pointed. "That means that way's west. And the lake's west of the road, because I saw it on the map. So if we just start after the sun and keep following, we ought to hit the road first, and the lake after that."

"Come on," said Jane.

A minute later the clearing was deserted. A possum

emerged from the trees and washed itself at the brook. But whether it had any wish in mind, and whether the magic was watered down below possum strength, too, will never be known, at least not by Jane and Mark and Katharine.

They were far away by now, crashing through the underbrush and following the sun, stopping every so often when Mark told them to so he could take his bearings.

They came out onto the red-clay road at last, farther from home than where they had left it. The lake wasn't even visible from here, and Mark decided the best plan was to head back toward their own field. Katharine counted seven hills before they reached their gate. Nobody had breath enough for much talking, but as they climbed the gate and went bumping over the field (little heeding whether the rams were unfriendly or not, this time), Jane managed to utter a few words between puffings.

"What'll we do when we get there?" she said. "Just wish?"

"What else?" gasped Mark. "We can't worry about consequences now. We've got to save her. No matter what."

"Let come what may," agreed Katharine.

The three children thudded across the hilly field, over the second gate, and through the yard of the cottage. Their mother sat reading on the porch. She looked up and saw Jane and Mark running, with Katharine trailing behind.

"Hello, darlings," she said. "Playing tag?"

Nobody answered. Snail shells crunched under their flying feet now, followed by the splud, splud of damp sand. A glance showed the lake, blue and ordinary and empty of magic menacings, before them.

"But that doesn't signify," said Jane. "Imagine what's probably underneath! Just lurking there!"

"Let's not," said Katharine.

Mark touched the lake first. "I wish we were on the island with Martha," was all he could say before breath utterly failed.

And then they were.

# 6. The Island

The next thing Martha knew after she made the wish, a salty breeze was lifting her hair, and she was standing on the rocks that rimmed the familiar coral island. Just before her were the four palm trees where she and the others had hidden on that first fateful magical day. She ran forward.

There, right in front of the four trees, was the flat stone, just as she remembered it, with Chauncey Cutlass's initials blazoned on its front. She flung herself on her knees and scrabbled in the sand with her fingers. Too late, she wished she had brought a shovel. Still, maybe one could be fetched by magical means.

Hurrying back to the rocks, Martha leaned over, plunged her finger in the water, and wished again. Nothing happened. So Mark must have been right that first day, and this tropic sea had no connection with the magic lake. Either that, or the salt got in the way of the magic current. "Like a short circuit," muttered Martha to herself, running back to the flat stone, "whatever that is."

If there were a tree-branch she could make a stick for digging! But the only trees were palm trees, and Martha felt that a palm leaf right now would be but as a broken reed. So she used her hands again.

At last she managed to get one end of the stone free of the encroaching sand (breaking several fingernails in the process). Huffing and puffing, she heaved the stone away and to one side. Beneath it was just more sand, heeled down and trampled well by the industrious pirates. Martha got to work on it. Her fingers were sore by now, and there seemed to be no end to the gritty graininess, except that as she got lower it got wetter and scratchier.

"I've heard of the sands of time," she said aloud, "and these must be it."

But a second later one hand struck solid metal, and a tantalizing corner of pirate-chest appeared at the bottom of the hole. Martha started to dig faster.

Then she stopped. All this while she had been half-hearing a sort of plashing sound in the water at her back. Probably just waves, she thought. But now the plashing was nearer and louder. Something made her turn and look behind her.

A long, canoe-shaped boat was fast approaching the island, manned by what looked like hundreds of black-skinned figures. A few strings of beads here and there formed their only costume. Their white teeth gleamed in the sun.

"Natives!" was Martha's first thought. "Friends or enemies?"

Probably the natives wouldn't notice, though, was her second thought. Probably they wouldn't any more than half-see her, the way the pirates had that other time, and probably they'd just think the island was haunted, and she could scare them away as easy as pie and get on with the digging.

As her mind spoke this thought, one of the natives stood up (rocking the boat) and pointed straight at her with his paddle. And a fierce battle cry went up from every dusky throat.

And Martha remembered that she had broken the rules

and wished there *weren't* any rules any more, and now there *weren't*. And here she was, alone and unprotected on a desert island, and *everybody* would notice. Particularly savages.

A weaker spirit might have quailed, or hid its head in the sand. Martha did neither. Her one concern now was to protect the treasure, and Mr. Smith and the bookshop. Huffing and puffing harder than ever, she dragged the flat stone back into place and started stamping it down.

Behind her she heard a boat-landing sound, followed by the thud of running feet. Then the running stopped, and the only sound was a sound of breathing. Whether it was her own or the savages', Martha wasn't sure. She decided to look around again.

She did, and quickly shut her eyes. But that was even worse, and she opened them once more. The bead-clad savages were standing in a ring around her. Some carried spears with jaggy-looking edges (if a spear can have an edge). All of them were looking straight at her, and she could read only utter unfriendliness in their gaze. And she could read something else, only she wasn't quite sure what it was. Or if it was what she was afraid it was, she hoped she was wrong.

She thought it time to address the islanders. "Ugh," she said. "Mugwump. Mattapan. Chop Suey."

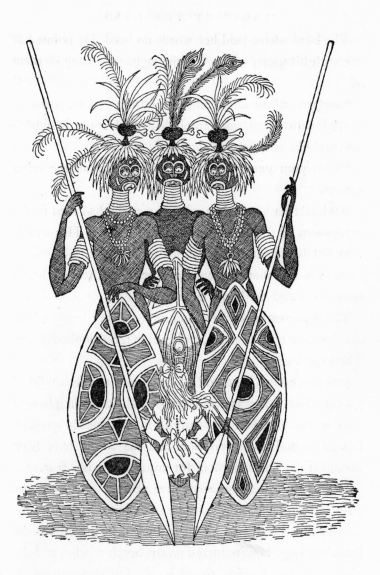

The head native paid her words no heed. He pointed at her with his spear, which was the jaggiest-looking of them all.

"Supperum," he said. "Smallum fattum girlum. Roastum stuffed with breadfruit crumbs. Custard apple in mouth all same like sucklingum piggum."

"Yum yum yummmmmmmmmmmm," said all the other natives.

And Martha knew then what it was she had seen in the expressions of the savage eyes. It was hunger. This was a cannibal island, and they were cannibals.

As this fell thought sank into her brain, rough hands seized her, and she knew no more.

When she came to, for a minute she didn't know where she was. She tried to move, and couldn't. She looked down. Then she knew.

She was bound hand and foot and tied to the handle of a long spear that was standing up with its point plunged deep in the sand. Her feet dangled high above the ground. It was an undignified position, and she would have been furious if she had had room for any feelings but fear.

Drums were beating somewhere nearby, and there was a sound of rough voices raised in something that was probably intended to be song. Martha looked. It was just as she feared. A huge bonfire blazed on the beach nearby, and the islanders were dancing round it, waving their spears. A vast caldron hung over the fire. Steam issued from it, and Martha knew only too well (from Katharine's home cooking lessons) that any minute it would come to a boil.

"O turtle!" she cried, trying to make her voice heard above the din.

Not a thing happened. Naturally. All rules were broken now, and there wouldn't be a soul to help her, and she was the one who had done it. It was only what she deserved, but that was small comfort.

The caldron began to bubble. Martha spared a second for a wish that if Jane and Mark and Katharine ever got out of the woods and arrived back at the magic lake and were noble enough to try to help her, it would be too late. After all, there was no point in their being boiled, too. Then she wept, a prey to despair.

Savage hands seized her, spear and all, and carried her toward the bonfire. She could feel its heat all around her now, and the steam from the caldron was warm and damp on her face.

Then, just at the moment when she was abandoning all hope, there was an interruption.

Three forms appeared on the island's rocky shore. The forms were those of Jane and Katharine and Mark. Because at just that moment they *had* arrived at the lake and made their wish, and it *wasn't* too late, and here they were.

Their horrified eyes took in the scene.

"What'll we do?" said Katharine.

"Pretend we're white gods from the sea, silly!" said Jane. "That's what explorers *always* do! It *always* works!"

"Wait," said Mark, wanting to stop and think it over, as usual.

"There's no time!" said Jane, and for once she was right about this, for the natives were holding Martha poised over the caldron now, and one of them was just reaching out to cut the bonds that held her to the spear and were all that kept her from the scalding depths below.

"Stop that!" cried Jane, striding forward and waving her arms as a great white goddess from the sea should. "Salaam! Hallelujah! Boria Boola Ga!"

Katharine tried to follow her example, but she couldn't think of anything godlike to say. "Vamoose! Twenty-three skidoo! Skat, you nasty things!" were the words that fell from her lips.

The cannibals jumped, startled, and some of them dropped their weapons. The ones who were holding Martha's spear let it fall (luckily to one side of the caldron, and Martha was only slightly bruised). Mark took advantage of the distraction to kick quite a lot of sand onto the bonfire. It went out. He reached down to pick up one of the weapons the savages had dropped.

But the cannibal chief wasn't to be discouraged so easily. He put his foot on the spear Mark was trying to pick up.

"Bushwah!" he said (or a native word that sounded very much like that). "Don't believum. White man always tell same old storyum. All same likum Captain Cook. Tellum native him great white goddum. Wasn't. Heap big fakum."

He rallied his flagging cohorts round him, and they started for Jane and Katharine menacingly. Mark ran forward to bar the way.

"Beware!" he cried wildly. "Great white goddum! Am, too! Prove it! Heap big magic! Fire magic! Voodoo!" And pulling out a box of matches he happened to have in his pocket, he struck one of them and brandished it in the cannibal chief's face.

The chief remained unimpressed. "Old stuffum," he said. "Modern invention. Safety matchum." And blowing out the match contemptuously, he seized Mark in his raven grip. Others of the savage horde laid hold of Jane and Katharine.

Mark fleetingly wished he were the Connecticut Yankee at the Court of King Arthur and could predict an eclipse of the sun, and then it would happen, and that would show them. But he wasn't, and he couldn't.

And the cannibal chief had probably had the book read out loud to him by some missionary, anyway, Mark reflected bitterly. And then he had probably eaten the missionary, coat and bands and hymnbook, too.

The only thing Mark *could* do was let himself be bound

hand and foot and tied to a spear like Martha before him. Out of the corner of one eye he could see Jane and Katharine being subjected to the same humiliating treatment. Five minutes later the four children were dangling from their four spears like so many sides of meat hanging in a butcher shop waiting to be roasted. Mark shuddered. Every idea he had seemed to lead back to the same horrid subject.

The natives were hurrying about below them now, gathering wood for another fire and hauling out three more caldrons (though how they had fitted four caldrons into their one narrow canoe Mark couldn't imagine).

"This is the worst thing that's happened to us *yet!*" cried Katharine from her spear.

"Don't give up. Keep thinking. We've always managed to find a way out before," called Mark, reassuringly from his, though he didn't really feel as hopeful as he tried to sound.

"We hadn't broken all the rules then, and ruined everything," said Jane, who was in no mood to consider the feelings of her youngest sister.

Martha gave way to tears again. I will not say whether any of the others joined her, or which ones.

The bonfires were nearly built now, and the caldrons being hung in place. But the natives were moving more slowly, and pausing every few moments to wipe their brows. The sun had climbed high in the heavens. It was hot. Some of the cannibals abandoned all pretense of work and flung themselves down on the sand and shut their eyes. Others followed their example.

"What's the matter with them?" said Jane. "Why don't they cook us now and get it over with? This suspense is awful."

"They're tired," said Katharine. "No wonder, after all that fire, and dancing, and then working in this heat. I feel as if I were cooked already."

A savage hurried up to the chief and said something. He pointed at the sun directly above. The chief nodded and cried out a word of command. All the cannibals immediately stopped whatever they were doing, and dropped whatever they held at the moment, be it stick or caldron (several toes were quite badly crushed), and flung themselves down wherever they happened to be. Slumber descended on their perspiring faces.

As for the chief, he curled himself up in the shade of a sheltering palm and began to snore. Two of the natives who seemed to be slaves propped a canopy over him and fanned the flies away for a bit, before going to sleep themselves.

"What is it?" said Katharine in the sudden silence.

"It's siesta time," said Mark. "All tropic tribes do it. They take naps every noon."

"Naps!" cried Jane. "I never thought I'd be glad to hear that word! I wish I could take one right now, and wake up and it was all a dream!"

"As if we could sleep at a time like this!" said Katharine.

But it's surprising what the tropical sun can do, particularly when you are tied to a spear in the full glare of it. First Katharine and then Jane gave way to its soporific rays and began to nod. Mark stayed awake for a while trying to think of a way out and not finding any; then he, too, lapsed into utter dozing. Horrible nightmares disturbed his rest, but he only twitched and muttered and slumbered on.

Only Martha remained sleepless, a prey to woe and remorse, promising herself that if they managed to escape this time—only she couldn't think how—she would never wish on a lake, or anything else, again.

A time passed.

The other three awoke to the sound of voices.

"Where am I?" said Katharine.

"Who's there?" said Mark.

"Three guesses," said Jane bitterly. "It's those natives. They're discussing whether they want us stewed or parboiled."

But it wasn't the natives.

"Look!" said Katharine, pointing. "It's Martha. Who in the world is she talking to?"

Jane and Mark looked. Sure enough, the natives were still all stretched out, motionless. Several of them were snoring loudly. And there, at the foot of Martha's spear, where it was plunged in the sand, stood three children. Only Jane and Mark couldn't see them very clearly. It was as though they were sort of *half* there, the way Martha had been once on a half-magic time, long ago.

Martha and the three strange children were making conversation, for all the world as though they weren't in the least peril at all.

"I'm seven years old," Martha was saying. "I'm in the second grade next year. My teacher's name is Miss Van Buskirk." All trace of tears or care had vanished from her voice.

"Honestly!" said Jane. "At a time like this! Who are you?" she added rudely, staring down at the three strange children.

"This one's called Ann," said Martha happily, pointing at the smaller girl, "and the boy's Roger and the big girl is Eliza. They're in a magic adventure, too, and our magics kind of overlapped. Isn't that interesting?"

"Oh, they are, are they?" said Jane, who was in no mood for trifling.

"Yes, we are. Did you think *you* had all the magic in

the world?" said the one called Eliza, proving that she could be just as rude as Jane.

"That's why we can't see you clearly, then," said Mark.

"Can't you?" said Martha. "*I* can."

"That's funny," said the one called Ann. "Roger and I can see *you* clearly, but Eliza can't."

"I can see *that* one," said the girl called Eliza, pointing at Katharine.

"I can see *you*, too," said Katharine, beaming at her. "Still, that's typical of that magic," she went on wisely. "You never can tell what it'll do." A new thought struck her. "Why, when you think of it, there're probably hundreds of children in the middle of hundreds of magics, wandering all over the world all the time! It's a wonder we don't meet more often. It's a wonder we don't have collisions! How did you happen to come *here?*"

The boy called Roger looked at the girl called Ann. "Why, we . . ." he started to say. But Katharine interrupted him, chattering on.

"I know. Of course. The turtle sent you."

"What turtle?" said the girl called Ann. So that couldn't be it.

"Oh, for heaven's sake!" fumed Jane. "What is this, a social tea? What does it matter how they got here? The point is, can they get us down?"

"Our magic only works for time," said the boy called Roger.

"Really?" said Jane, feeling superior. "Ours works for *everything!*" Then she remembered. "Only right now it isn't working at all," she admitted. "That is, it's working, but it's all gone wrong."

"That happens to us sometimes, too," said Roger.

"Pooh!" said the dashing one called Eliza. "We don't need any old magic to get them off those spears. We have our two hands, don't we? And our crude childish strength?" And digging in the sand suddenly, she uprooted Jane's spear, and Jane fell heavily to the ground, knocking all the wind out of her. She always maintained afterwards that Eliza had done it on purpose. But whether or not this was true, it was also true that once she had brought Jane to earth, Eliza worked just as hard as anyone else at undoing her bonds.

The boy called Roger let Mark down more gently and went to work on the ropes that held *him*. As soon as he and Jane were untied, they and Roger and Eliza attended to Katharine and Martha.

"Free at last," said Katharine, rubbing her chafed wrists.

"And with no help of turtle," said Jane. "Stuck-up thing. We'll show him."

Martha said nothing. So far, so good. Maybe they were going to get home unscathed, after all.

"How did you get here in the first place?" asked the little girl called Ann.

"We were after buried treasure, and the cannibals caught us," said Katharine.

"That's right, the cannibals," said Mark, looking round at the slumberous natives. "I was almost forgetting. We'd better talk softly."

"Do you get captured by cannibals *often?* I never have, so far," said the Eliza one in rather an envious voice. "What about the treasure? Can we help you find it? Where's it buried?"

An unworthy thought troubled the mind of Mark, and from looking at Jane he could see that she was thinking the same thing. If these nice strange children helped them find the treasure, maybe they would have to share it with them, and that would mean so much less for Mr. Smith and the bookshop. Still, seven heads (and fourteen hands) were better than four (or eight). And besides, it would be only fair.

"Shall we tell them?" Jane's eyes spoke to Mark.

"Yes," Mark signaled back. "Follow me," he said aloud. "Better be careful. Walk tiptoe."

Quite a lengthy procession crossed the sand. Mark heaved away the flat stone, and then paused on the brink of the hole Martha had dug.

"We'd better figure out first how we're going to get away afterwards," he said.

"And if we *can*," agreed Jane. "Those natives might wake up any minute." She turned to the three strange children. "How does your magic work? Do you say spells? Or do you have something with you? Some magic coin or something?"

"We have *something*," admitted the boy called Roger. And he took *something* carefully from his pocket. Mark and Jane and Katharine and Martha couldn't see clearly what it was, though Jane stood on her tiptoes and peered. She said afterwards that it looked just like some old pieces of grass to *her*, but of course it must have been more than that. Anyway, as they all afterwards agreed, it certainly was *something!*

"We have this," the boy Roger went on, "but it only works for time, the way I told you."

"It gets us back to our own time when we're finished," said Ann.

"Maybe it'd get *you* back to *yours*, at the same time," said Eliza. "Only it *wouldn't* be the same time, if you see what I mean."

"Clear as mud," said Jane.

"*I* get it," said Mark. "You mean maybe it'd take us back to *your* time with *you*, instead."

133

"That's what I'm worried about," said Roger.

"What if it does?" said Jane. "We could rest up, and then go on from there."

The boy Roger shook his head doubtfully. "You wouldn't like it," he said. "It wouldn't work out. You wouldn't fit in."

"Why?" said Katharine. "What time *is* it?"

"It's later than we think," said Mark, studying the sky anxiously. "It's getting to be afternoon. We'd better hurry. Those cannibals'll wake up any minute. If they do, we'll just have to take a chance."

Seven heads turned to the treasure hole, and fourteen hands set to work. All dug hard, but none dug harder than Jane and Eliza. In next to no time at all, the same corner of chest appeared at the bottom of the hole, just as it had for Martha.

Now there was a difference of opinion. Mark, ever cautious, and Roger, who seemed to be of the same temperament, wanted to keep digging till the chest was all uncovered and get it out whole. Jane and Eliza wanted to scrape the sand away from the rest of the lid and open it and look inside first.

"How do we know? Maybe it's all a hoax," said Jane. "It'd be just like that Chauncey Cutlass."

"Who's he?" said Ann.

"Never mind. Let's be digging," said Eliza. She and Jane won by sheer dint of getting in the way of any who tried to dig in a different direction.

The four corners of the chest-lid appeared. Jane laid hold of them and pulled.

"Maybe it's locked," said Katharine.

But it wasn't. The lid flew back on its hinges. Everybody took one look and gasped.

Pieces of eight were inside, and jewels, just as Mark had predicted. Diamonds glittered in necklace-y coils, and emeralds and rubies and sapphires and other stones nobody knew the names of but that were just as pretty and probably just as precious. There was enough to divide and still have plenty to save more than one faltering bookshop.

"We'll go halves," said Jane nobly to Eliza. "There's probably somebody *you* could help, too."

"Let's start," said Eliza. "You take a diamond necklace and I'll take a diamond necklace; you take a ruby ring and I'll take a ruby ring. . . ."

Two eager hands reached out and down.

And at that moment the cannibal chief woke up.

He took a look around, rubbed his eyes, and took another. He saw the seven children, and his eyes flashed fire. "Wah!" he cried. "Samoa! Goona goona!"

All the cannibals immediately woke up, reached for

their weapons, and scrambled to their feet. Their teeth gleamed hungrily as they saw three extra children for dinner, and their faces lighted with avarice as they beheld the pirate's treasure, for gold is gold no matter where you find it. They rushed forward, spears in hand.

"Quick!" cried Mark to Roger. "Make the wish! *Any* time's better than this one!"

Roger clutched whatever it was he had in his hand tight, and muttered something. Jane and Mark and Katharine and Martha were never sure afterwards what he said. But whatever it was, it did the trick.

The next thing they knew, the four children were standing on their own beach by their own lake. There was no sign of the cannibals and no sign of the treasure, and there was no sign of the strange children called Roger and Ann and Eliza, either.

But their mother was there, sitting in a deck chair, on the sand, and because all rules were broken, she saw them appear out of the everywhere into the here perfectly plainly, and the four children had a terrible time explaining to her how they had done it so that she wouldn't think her mind was giving way, the way she had one time before.

"We were in the maple tree on the bank, and we all jumped down," said Mark, crossing his fingers behind his back.

"You couldn't. It's too high," said their mother, looking at the tree.

"We did, though," said Jane, crossing *her* fingers.

"Then you shouldn't have," said their mother. "How many times do I have to tell you. . . ."

The speech that began with these familiar words went on for quite some time. The four children listened patiently. At the end of it, their mother went into the cottage, still looking from the tree to the beach and shaking her head despairingly. The four children were alone and could discuss really serious matters.

"Why didn't you grab some of that treasure before he wished?" said Martha to Jane. "Even one necklace would have helped Uncle Huge."

"I couldn't," said Jane. "It happened too fast."

"At least we know it's there now," said Katharine, ever the peacemaker. "We can go back for it next time."

"If there *is* any next time, after what you did," said Jane to Martha accusingly. "You'll have a lot of explaining to do to that turtle. It probably won't ever speak to us again. You've probably just ruined the whole thing utterly and completely."

"Except if all rules are broken and the lake's full of magic," Mark reminded them, "we could probably wish for anything any old time."

"Only not right now," said Katharine hastily.

"And we'd better clear it with the turtle anyway, just in case," Mark decided.

"Still," said Martha after a pause, "I'm sort of glad I did it, in a way. If I hadn't, we probably wouldn't ever have met those other children. I liked them."

"I liked the Eliza one," said Katharine. "She was fun."

"I wonder where they are now," said Jane.

"I wonder if we'll ever see them again," said Martha.

"Children," said their mother from the porch. "Come help get supper."

So they did.

## 7. The Treasure

The next morning after breakfast (and after bedmaking, dishwashing, and other dull details, but I prefer not to mention them, as who wouldn't?), the four children went down to the shore. Martha didn't want to go, but the others made her.

The turtle was waiting on the beach with wrath in its eye.

"Well?" it said.

"I know," said Martha. "I'm sorry. At least," she went on, feeling that she ought to be truthful, "I'm sorry for what I did, but I'm glad I met those children. Will we ever see them again?"

139

"That," said the turtle, "would be telling. And now is not the time. What did I tell you about considering that lake's feelings?"

"You told us to wish wet wishes," said Martha with a hint of rebellion, "and I did."

"Humph!" said the turtle. "A wish out of season's just as bad as a lake out of water. You've heard about disturbing the balance of nature. Well, magic has a balance, too, and when you break the rules, you upset it. I told you once that lake's stronger than I am now. And now you've got it all upset, there's no telling what it might do next!"

"You mean the magic might dry *up?*" said Jane.

"Either that," said the turtle darkly, "or the other extreme."

What the other extreme from drying up might be, no one liked to think. Explode, probably, or come running up the bank and overflow. The four children had heard of flood disasters, and a *magic* flood disaster would probably be even worse. Martha thought of the big snake thing they had seen and trembled.

"You mean it's all over?" said Mark. "We can't wish any more?"

"I think," said the turtle, "that it would be much safer not to."

"Who cares about safe?" said Jane recklessly. "We've

*got* to! We've got to find that treasure. Now we know it's there."

"Why?" said the turtle.

They told it. They told it all about Mr. Smith, and the bookshop, and about business being bad, and all Mr. Smith had done for them, and how much they wanted to help him in return.

The turtle (so far as could be seen, what with the shell) relaxed a little, as it heard their story. "Hmmmm," it said, when they had finished. "Good intentions again. Sometimes I think they're worse than the other kind. Still," it added thoughtfully, "you never can tell with magic. It might take that into consideration if I went and explained to it. It might think the end justified the means. Though *that*," the turtle went on, with a severe look at them all, "is a highly dangerous doctrine and one I shouldn't think of recommending to you mere mortals. Why, you could justify *anything* that way!"

"I *know!*" said Katharine wisely. "Wars and conquest!"

"Exactly!" said the turtle. "Look at Napoleon! But that's another story." It broke off and studied them with its cold, hooded gaze. "I wonder," it said, "exactly how much you want to help this friend of yours. Would you do it if it meant your last wish?"

"Our last wish on the lake," said Mark, "or our last wish ever?"

"It might even come to that," said the turtle.

All eyes met, and all hearts sank for a moment. But all spirits were steadfast.

"Yes," said Mark. The three others nodded.

"Then I'll see what I can do," said the turtle. "I'll go speak to that magic. I'll put it up to it man to man, as you might say."

"What do we do in the meantime?" said Jane.

The turtle looked at her. "I haven't the least idea," it said coldly. "What do you *usually* do?" And it turned to go.

"Wait!" said Mark. "At least tell us when to expect it! If it happens at all, I mean. Because if we aren't prepared, we might make a mistake again, and it would be awful to waste our one chance!"

The turtle's gaze softened. "The only way I know to straighten out a mess like this," it said, "is to go back to the beginning and start over."

"With the same old rules?" said Katharine.

"Every third day?" said Martha.

The turtle eyed her. "*I* always thought that a very sensible arrangement myself," it said. "It was good enough for me and my father before me. Not to mention sundry enchanters of eld."

"Then it'll happen day after tomorrow," said Jane.

"Don't count on it," said the turtle. And it walked into the water and swam away.

The rest of that day and all the next one passed uneventfully. A few good things happened, like driving in to Angola to see chapter seven of Ruth Roland in *Ruth of the Rockies*, and the time Mark saw a bird that wasn't in his small bird book, and Mr. Smith brought a big important one home from the bookshop and Mark looked it up and it turned out to be a blue-gray gnatcatcher, which is very rare, at least at an Indiana lake. This wasn't very interesting to anyone but Mark, but then there is nothing so boring as bird-watching, except to those people to whom it isn't boring at all.

And otherwise little happened that was worth recording, and little was said that needs repetition. The third day dawned neither very good nor very bad. It wasn't the kind of sunny singing morning when miracles seem made to happen, but it wasn't the kind of dun-gray day that discourages all hope, either. Clouds ringed the sky, but there were bright intervals.

The four children assembled on the beach rather late, wanting to give the magic every opportunity and not rush it. No one breathed a word of the question that was in all hearts. No one had to ask what the wish was going to be. No one but Mark even spoke. He marched straight to the water's edge, and Jane took one of his hands and Katharine took the other, and Martha joined on at one end.

"I wish," said Mark, "that we would find the buried treasure."

Immediately everyone gasped for breath, and a great wind seemed to blow away the world, as it so often does when you wish to be taken somewhere by magic and it happens.

"It worked!" said Martha, when the wind stopped and she could catch her breath.

"You didn't say *what* buried treasure!" said Jane to Mark. "You didn't wish we could *keep* it, either!"

"What does that matter?" said Katharine. "We're here."

"Yes, but where?" said Mark, looking around. "This isn't our island."

And it wasn't. Instead of the well-known sand and sparse palm trees, lush vegetation met the four children's gaze. The trees hung with ripe fruits, rare flowers laid their scent upon the breeze, and pure, clear streams coursed everywhere. A sky of a peculiarly bright blue canopied the scene. Beyond some rocks, a sea of a deeper blue lay dreamily becalmed. It was an island all right, but it wasn't theirs.

"I knew it!" said Jane, glaring at Martha. "The magic

144

couldn't do it. It tried, but it wasn't up to it. It's been through too much. And it's all your fault."

"I know," said Martha, hanging her head.

"Wait," said Mark. "It may not be so bad. There may be buried treasure here, too. There must be, or it wouldn't have brought us here."

"Unless it's getting even!" said Jane.

Everyone felt a clutch of fear at these dark words— everyone but Katharine, who didn't hear them. She had wandered away and was busily exploring.

"Anyway, it's a wet wish," said Mark, pointing at the sea around them. "That's a good sign. You'd think."

Katharine came running back. "I've been here before!" she said. "At least it feels as if. It's all sort of familiar. Like a book I read or something!"

"Maybe it's *Treasure* Island," said Mark. "Maybe we'll see Jim Hawkins!"

"And Long John Silver, and match wits with him!" said Jane, who had always wanted to try.

"No," said Katharine. "It's not *that* exactly. But it's on that order." She broke off, and looked around again. "I know," she said. "It's like a *picture* in a book. The way those rocks are, and that blue sky. It's like a picture by the man that did the one in my room. The amfalula tree picture!"

"Maxfield Parrish," said Mark, who always knew the facts.

"I guess so," said Katharine. "What book of his do we have? Something kind of oriental."

Light dawned on Jane. "*The Arabian Nights!*" she cried. "We're in Arabian Night country!"

And all the others agreed, as they studied the landscape, that an Arabian Night was exactly what it looked like, except that right now it was daytime.

"What island is there in that?" said Katharine.

"Don't you remember?" said Mark. "Sinbad the Sailor! And the roc's egg!"

Everyone took another look around. Sure enough, there, poised on a cliff not far away, was an enormous round white object.

"Well? What do we do now?" said Martha.

"Wait for the roc to come down, of course," said Jane, "and then fly away with it. If Sinbad could do it, we can!"

Even as she spoke, an immense cloud darkened the sun.

"Here it comes now!" Jane went on. "Hurry up! We tie ourselves to its claws and then it carries us away!"

"There's no treasure in that story," objected Katharine, hurrying along with Jane and the others just the same.

"There is, too. There's the ground all covered with diamonds and serpents," said Jane.

"Ugh!" said Martha, stopping in her tracks and refusing to go another inch.

"Don't worry, it won't be that," Mark told her. "That's not *buried* treasure, and we asked for *buried*. The magic couldn't get it *that* wrong."

"I don't care!" said Jane. "We're supposed to catch on, just the same. I *know* we are. Otherwise it wouldn't be here. It all works out. Maybe it'll take us somewhere else. Maybe it'll take us to our own island!"

Martha let herself be persuaded, and the four children arrived at the roc's egg just as the giant bird alighted over the egg and, crouching down, spread its wings and brooded over it, and composed itself to sleep.

Mark started walking round the roc, observing it from all sides and making mental notes for his bird-watching book, but Jane was impatient.

"Don't waste time!" she said. "It may be leaving any minute!"

So Mark tied himself to one fabulous claw, like Sinbad before him, only Mark used the belt of his blue jeans. The three girls bound themselves on with their hair ribbons, all except Martha, who had lost hers. She used Jane's long white socks instead.

Then, ready for anything, the four children waited for the roc to wake up and fly away. Nothing happened.

"If there's one thing I haven't any use for," said Jane, after what felt like two hours at *least* had passed, "it's a bird. You and your blue-gray gnatcatchers!" And she directed a withering look at Mark.

But at long last the roc awoke and, with a loud cry, rose from the egg. The children rose with it. Martha gave a loud cry, too.

But after the first few sickening moments, the sensation was lovely, and the four children studied the scene below with interest. At first there was just heaving sea, but then a rocky coast appeared.

"Island ahoy!" said Mark.

But it wasn't an island. It was a vast continent that went on and on as the roc flew inland, over field and forest.

"Where's it taking us?" said Martha.

"Somewhere in some other Arabian Night, I suppose," said Jane. And a city full of mosques and minarets appeared below, just to prove it.

"I'll sing thee songs of Araby," breathed Katharine romantically, looking down, "and tales of far Cashmere."

"Don't," said Martha. "Not at a time like this. I couldn't stand it." Even as she spoke, the city below gave way to another forest.

A sudden thought struck Mark. "I know!" he said. "Of course! Where in *The Arabian Nights* is there buried treasure? Well, *sort* of buried," he corrected himself. "Under ground, anyway."

Before the others could guess, the roc slackened pace and began circling lower and lower.

"Does it know it's got passengers?" said Martha. "Will it stop and let us off?"

"I'm not sure," said Mark. "Better get ready for an emergency landing."

He started loosening the belt that held him to the great claws, and the girls went to work on their hair-ribbons (and socks).

For only an instant the roc hovered low over a clearing in the forest. The four children had barely time to get free and jump before it sailed away again. They landed lightly on soft leaf-mold.

"Thanks a lot," called Martha after their departing guide. The roc did not reply.

"Where are we?" said Katharine, picking herself up.

"Don't you know?" said Mark, on his feet now and pointing.

Everybody looked.

Before them was a huge rock, so steep and craggy that it was almost a mountain.

Mark didn't hesitate. He walked straight up to the rock, opened his mouth, and just before he spoke light dawned, and everybody else knew what two words he would say.

The two words were, "Open, Sesame!"

Immediately the expected happened. A door in the rock opened. Beyond it yawned a vast cavern.

"It's the cave Ali Baba found. It's the cave of the Forty Thieves. It's *that* buried treasure!" said Mark, as though anybody needed telling now. "Come on!" He hurried forward, and everybody else followed. Martha hung back, but the others pushed her. As soon as they were inside, the door shut, of itself. Martha wished it wouldn't. But she looked round at what the cave contained and oh'ed and ah'ed with the others, just the same.

There were all sorts of provisions, rich bales of silk stuff, brocade, and valuable carpeting, piled upon one another, gold and silver pieces in great heaps, and ancient Arabian coins in bags.

"What'll we take?" said Jane.

"Ought we?" said Katharine.

"Of course. Ali Baba did, didn't he? It's all right to rob robbers!"

"Money!" suggested Martha simply.

"Better not," said Mark. "You never can tell with currency. It might be debased by the time we get it back home."

"What's that?" said Martha.

"Not good any more," said Jane. "Better concentrate on jewels and precious metals. They *always* come in handy."

So she and Mark and Martha sat down on the floor of the cave and started to make a pile of handy things to take home.

"Gold pieces for Mr. Smith," said Mark, starting to sort these out from the silver.

"And jewels for Mother," said Jane, pointing to a heap of diamonds and rubies no one else had noticed.

"What about these carpets?" said Katharine, tugging at a pile of rugs. "One of them might be a magic one. We could sail home in style! And it'd be useful for later on, if the lake magic's really worn out after this wish."

"Too risky," Mark decided. "We couldn't find out if it's magic or not without sitting on it and wishing to be somewhere, and then it'd probably *take* us there, and we'd probably get all involved in some other adventure and probably never get back to find the treasure at all!"

And from their experiences in the past, the others could not but agree that this was probably only too likely.

"Put that carpet *down!*" said Jane to Katharine. "You don't know where it might *go!*" Katharine moved on, exploring.

Mark dumped the money out of one of the bags, filled

the bag with gold pieces and jewels, put a few of the coins back in for his coin collection, and pulled the drawstrings. "Well," he said, "I guess that's it. Might as well start for home."

But they didn't.

"Psst! Lookit!" came a voice at that moment. The voice was Katharine's, and it came from deeper in the cave. "Come here!" she called, and the others went there, Mark carrying the bag of treasure. They looked where Katharine pointed.

"Oil jars!" she was saying excitedly. "Thirty-eight of 'em. I counted. They're the jars the robbers hide in when they try to kill Ali Baba!"

"But that doesn't come into the story till later," objected Jane, "after they've found out Ali Baba's been taking their treasure and they try to get even!"

"They'd have to store them somewhere in the meantime, wouldn't they?" said Katharine. "They've probably just reached that part of the story, and this is where we came in! Anyway, there they are!"

And there they were, thirty-eight perfectly ordinary Arabian Night oil jars made of goatskin standing in a neat row in the depths of the cave.

"Sure, that's probably it," Mark figured it out. "They've probably just bought the oil jars, and tonight the robber chief'll take them to Ali Baba's house with the thieves hidden inside them, and then in the story they're supposed to jump out and kill everybody, only that slave girl thwarts them!"

"Maybe there's thieves hiding in them right now!" said Jane.

"Let's go home," said Martha.

"Wait," said Katharine. And daringly standing on tiptoe, she peeked into one of the jars. But it was empty. And so were all the others when they looked, except one that was full of oil, for the appearance of things.

"We'd better hurry, though," said Mark. "They may be here any minute."

"Wait," said Katharine, again. "I wonder how it feels hiding in one of those things. I've always wanted to find out." And before anyone could stop her, she had climbed on a convenient chest and was easing herself down through the neck of the nearest jar. "Plenty of room inside." Her voice came to them hollowly. "It smells of salad dressing, though."

"Come out!" called Martha beseechingly.

"Just a minute," said Katharine's voice. There was a scrabbling sound, followed by a silence. When she spoke again, she didn't sound so daring. "I can't!" she said. "I can't catch hold. It's slippery, and it sort of *gives!*"

"How did the robbers get out in the story?" said Jane.

"They used a knife, and cut their way through," said Mark. "Who's got a knife?"

Nobody had one.

Fate chose this moment to bring a sound of chinking and clanking from outside, as of many people mounted upon mules. A voice cried out something. The four children couldn't hear what it said, but it sounded all too much like two fateful, and familiar, words.

"Somebody do something!" cried Martha. "It's those thieves! They've come back! They're opening Sesame!"

Mark jumped up on the chest and tried to grab Katharine's hand to pull her out, but he couldn't get any purchase.

From behind them came a sound of rock scraping upon rock as the door of the cave started opening once again.

"It's too late!" said Mark to Katharine. "Scrooch down. Maybe they won't notice. Maybe they'll only half-see us, like the pirates that other time. It stands to reason, now we've got the rules back."

He and Jane and Martha hid behind a pile of rich brocades. Katharine scrooched down. The robber chief stalked into the cave, followed by thirty-seven bloodthirsty henchmen. (The other two of the forty thieves had already come to no good end earlier in the story.)

The chief took a look around the cave and smote one fist against the other. "By Allah!" he roared. "Someone has been here meddling again! See the gold pieces all every which way, and the diamonds dispersed and the rubies rearranged! Do I have to find our treasure tampered with every time I come in here? Probably that miserable Ali Baba butting in once more! But we shall give him bastinadoes and send him to Gehenna before this day is done, or know the reason why!"

"Please, O all-highest," said one of the thieves, investigating the pile of rugs. "The magic carpet has been tampered with, too!"

"You see?" hissed Jane to Mark, behind the pile of brocade. "It *was* magic. Don't you wish now we'd sat on it?"

"*I* do," said Martha, "and we wouldn't be here now."

"Shush," said Mark.

"No matter," said the bandit chief. "He shall rue the day. Our plans are laid. Man your oil jars. Boot, saddle, to mule, and away!"

"Oh, dear," said one of the robbers, looking at the oil jars apprehensively. "I always get so nervous in an enclosed space. I don't think I can go through with it, really I don't!"

"You know your duty, Abdul," said the chief sternly. "Man that oil jar!"

"At least let me practice first," said Abdul. And screwing up his courage, he marched to his appointed jar (which happened to be the one in which Katharine sat scrooched). He laid hold of the jar. He leaned over and peered within. Then he gave a cry, and leaped at least ten feet away, and fell on his face, pointing in the direction of Mecca. "Allah defend us!" he cried. "It be already occupied! It be haunted by an evil spirit!"

"Fie!" said the bandit chief. "More likely 'tis *you* who be haunted by the spirit of overmuch date wine! What did this evil spirit look like?"

"All small it was," said Abdul, "and the light shone through it."

"You see?" whispered Mark to Jane. "They *can* just half-see us!"

"And its face," continued Abdul with a shudder, "was that of a perfect fiend!"

"Why, you!" said Katharine, within the oil jar.

"Hark!" cried the terrified Abdul. "It speaks!"

The chief thief paled for a moment. Then he rallied. "Fie on you for a cowardly yoghourt," he said. "Probably a mere genie. You've heard of a genie in a bottle, haven't you? Then why not a genie in an oil jar, I should like to know? This is luck! Now it will do our bidding, and we can thwart that Ali Baba all the better and probably never

have to leave home at all!" He marched straight over to Katharine's hiding place. "Genie, genie," he said, "come out of your jar."

Katharine's heart thumped. This was her big moment, and she knew it, and yet what could she do? The proper thing, of course, would be to issue forth in a cloud of smoke and grow into a figure ten feet tall, and start doing magic tricks right and left. But she couldn't even climb out, let alone issue.

"I'm coming," she said, playing for time. "Just a minute." Once more she tried to catch hold of the slippery sides of the jar, and wished with all her heart that the lake *wasn't* worn out and the magic would aid them just once more.

"How the jar trembles!" cried Abdul, with another shudder.

"Hmmmmm," commented the chief, beginning to look skeptical. "A peculiar genie. It seems to be stuck. Never in a thousand and one nights have I seen the like!"

At that moment something pressed against Katharine, and a voice spoke in her ear.

"Move over," said the voice.

Katharine turned as far as she could in her cramped position. Scrunched against her in the narrow jar was a figure. I shall not attempt to describe what it looked like. Suffice it to say that it was a genie.

"Oh, good!" said Katharine. "I was just wishing something like you would turn up. Now you can fix everything. Did the turtle send you?"

"Not directly," said the genie, "but there are certain lines of communication among us magic beings. It sent out an SAS."

"You mean SOS," said Katharine.

"I do not," said the genie. " 'Send A Sorcerer' is the complete expression. 'Send O Sorcerer' would be nonsense!"

"How the genie mutters!" said the chief thief.

"Who's she talking to?" hissed Jane to Mark in their hiding place.

"More mutterings!" said the chief.

"Now that you're here, what are you going to do?" said Katharine to the genie. "Burst out and kill them all?"

"Certainly not," said the genie. "That would be interfering with the story. They have to go on and try to murder Ali Baba, just the way the book says. Changing that would be against the rules."

"But maybe if you just *scared* them a little," said Katharine, "then maybe they'd reform, and there wouldn't have to be *any* killing. And there'd be thirty-eight souls saved for Paradise. I should think you'd like that. I should think it'd be worth the effort."

"Hmmmmm," said the genie. "There may be something in what you say. Let me think it over for a minute."

159

There was a pause.

"I for one," said the bandit chief, "am getting tired of this waiting. I'm beginning to think there isn't any genie in there at all."

"Mayhap whoever was meddling with our treasure is hiding there, instead," said one of the thirty-seven henchmen.

"Mayhap 'tis Ali Baba himself, and now he's our prisoner," said another.

"It didn't *look* like him," said Abdul, "unless he's shrunk." But the others paid him no heed.

"Whoever it is," said the chief thief, "we shall give him a surprise. Fetch the jar with the oil and pour it in and suffocate him. *That* should teach him, genie or not!"

Ready feet ran to get the jar, and ready hands raised it to the waiting brim.

"It seems to me," said Katharine in the jar, "it's time to do something."

"I could not agree with you more," said the genie. "Suffocate *me*, would they? That settles it! Watch this!"

And a cloud of smoke enveloped him, and he sailed out of the jar in its midst and grew to at least twelve feet tall before the startled eyes of the thirty-eight thieves. And in some way that Katharine never afterwards figured out, the genie carried her along on the smoke with him. The smoke made a soft seat, though it was rather warm and steamy underneath.

"There," said the genie, depositing Katharine safely on the floor of the cave. He turned to glare at the robbers, and even their chief quailed.

"Well, genie," he said, trying to put up a show of bravado. "Have you come to do my bidding?"

"I certainly have not!" said the genie. "On your knees, villains!"

Mark and Jane and Martha ran out of their hiding place and joined Katharine, watching to see what would happen next.

"What did I tell you? It *is* an evil spirit!" cried Abdul. "And four imps with him!"

And he and the chief and all the bandits flung themselves flat, little heeding whether they faced Mecca or not, and rubbed their faces in the dirt in terror.

And then and there the genie began to teach the thieves such a lesson as they had never before had.

Invisible hands seized them and put them across invisible knees and gave them bastinadoes until they howled aloud for mercy. Thunder roared and lightning crackled. Earthquakes shook the cave, and great cracks opened in its floor. Through it all the laughter of the genie sounded with the voice of a hundred tornadoes. Jane and Mark and Katharine and Martha jumped up and down and shouted with excitement.

At last a final bolt of lightning ripped off the whole top of the cave, and the blue Arabian sky showed through from above. Rocks rolled and bounced all about, but the four children were unhurt (though many a thief was bruised black and blue).

Then came a sudden silence like the calm after a storm. Dust settled thickly. The howls of the robbers died away to exhausted whimpers.

"Well?" said the genie. "*Now* are you sorry?"

"Yes, yes, yes," cried all thirty-eight thieves.

"And you've reformed? And you'll never be robbers any more? And you'll let Ali Baba alone after this?"

"Even so! By Allah! Cross my heart!" cried the thieves.

"Very well, then," said the genie. He turned to the four children. "Are you ready to leave?"

"Sure," said Mark, catching up the bag of treasure.

"This was keen," said Jane. "All this, and treasure, and a good deed, too!"

"Brace yourselves," said the genie.

There was a whoosh, and the cave disappeared, and once again Katharine felt the strange sensation of traveling on the genie's smoke, and the other three felt it for the first time, and the next thing the four of them knew, they felt sand and snail shells underfoot, and they were staring at their own magic lake, and it was still morning.

When the smoke had cleared away, back in the robbers' cave, the chief robber looked around cautiously. Then he got to his feet.

"Well?" he said to his prostrate men. "What are you all doing down there on the floor? You look ridiculous."

The other robbers scrambled up hastily.

"There was a genie," said Abdul dazedly. "We made a promise. We reformed."

"I don't know what you're talking about," said the chief. "You must have been dreaming. *I* never saw any such thing. I never made any such promise, either. Catch *me!* Did any of *you* see anything?" And he looked round at his men threateningly.

The men were groaning and rubbing the parts of them that ached from the bastinadoes (and the falling rock). Now they stopped quickly. "Who? Us?" they said. "Certainly not. Not very likely. We never saw no such thing, neither!" And they all shook their heads solemnly.

"Very well," said the bandit chief. "Then get to work. Tote those jars. Harness those mules!"

And the thieves hefted up the oil jars, and got on their mules, and rode away to try to kill Ali Baba (and get killed themselves in the process), just as though nothing had happened. Which proves that the genie was right in the first place, and it's never any use trying to interfere with stories and make them end differently, because the way they ended in the first place is the way they're *supposed* to end.

And the genie was spoken to severely by his superiors, when he got back to headquarters, for forgetting it.

Meanwhile, on the shore of the lake, four minds had but a single thought, and four forms flung themselves down on the beach, and Mark undid the drawstrings of the bag and poured the shining treasure out upon the sand.

For an instant the bright gold and the red and white gems sparkled in the morning sun; then they seemed to suffer a change.

"What's happening?" said Jane in alarm. "It's all sort of melting!"

It was true. Every piece of gold and every diamond or ruby was shifting and sliding within itself, only instead of melting down to a liquid, they were flaking into dustlike grains that held their color for a moment and then went all lackluster and dead and earth-colored as they trickled away to mingle with the sands of the lake shore.

"It's chemistry!" said Mark. "They were buried too long, and we exposed them to the air too quickly. They couldn't stand it. Their molecules gave way!"

"It's that magic!" said Jane. "It could have held them to-gether if it really tried. It's working against us."

"Can't we save the pieces?" said Katharine. "Even the littlest bit of gold ought to be worth *something!*"

"We'd never find them," said Mark. "They're part of the dust of ages by now."

"There's some money, still," said Martha, pointing.

And sure enough, the ancient Arabic coins had survived transplanting and lay looking dull and uninteresting on the beach.

"What about *them?*" said Katharine. "They must be from awfully long ago. They ought to be worth a fortune by this time. Maybe they're the real treasure we're sup-posed to find!"

But when Mark ran and got his rare coin catalogue from the cottage and looked them up, it turned out they were the commonest ancient Arabic coins there were, and they weren't worth anything at all hardly.

And they weren't magic talismans, either, because the four children held each one in turn and wished, and noth-ing went on happening.

"Honestly!" said Jane. "That's the last time I'll even *speak* to that magic!"

"Better not say that," said Mark. "You may be more right than you know. Remember what the turtle said!"

And they all remembered.

"You mean it's really over?" said Katharine. "I don't believe it. It wouldn't all end like this. What would be the point? Why, we didn't learn a moral lesson, or anything! Even *that* would be better than nothing. So far as I can see, we might just as well not have gone at all!"

"You found out what hiding in an oil jar is like," Martha reminded her.

"And there was the genie," said Mark, "and flying. I guess I'm just about the only living bird-watcher who ever watched a roc. I may take up aviation when I grow up," he added thoughtfully. "I think it's here to stay."

"The bastinadoes were lovely!" gloated Jane. "Anyway, it may all come right. That's the way that magic is. It's like some people. It never does what you *want* it to exactly, but it's never been really *mean* before. Somehow it always works out in the end."

"I wouldn't count on it," said Mark.

There was a silence.

"Still," said Katharine, "we can't help hoping, can we?"

And somehow, in the long un-magic days that followed, they couldn't.

## 8. The End

The long un-magic days that followed were horrible at first, because the four children couldn't help waiting for the third day to see if anything would happen, and then when nothing did, they couldn't help waiting for the *third* third day (which ought to have been twice as magic, or even *cubed* as much). And when nothing happened *then*, all hope was despaired of, but after that things began to settle down into the normal lake-y routine.

Picnics were had, and walks were taken. Motorboat rides were even enjoyed. Mr. Smith taught Mark and Jane to paddle the canoe. Mark went on with his bird-watching and became quite knowledgeable about the least bittern. Katharine and Martha started a butterfly collection, only Katharine was always too tender-hearted and let the butterflies out of the net again after she'd caught them. (Martha, of course, knew no mercy.)

As for swimming, it never palled, in spite of the dire irony that there they were, plashing about day after day in a lake that was full of the most spine-tingling enchantments, and yet they couldn't break through to get in touch with any of them.

"Just think," said Jane to Mark one day as he was practicing the Australian crawl. "Nixies and Rhine maidens may be gamboling in this very same foam right now. They may be even touching us, for all we know. That frog over there might be the Frog Footman."

"Or the Frog Prince," said Katharine.

"Or Mr. Jeremy Fisher," said Martha.

"Stop it," said Mark. "Let sleeping frogs lie." And for the most part they did.

But ever and anon one of them would notice one of the others dipping his finger in the lake and muttering something, and then looking disappointed. And once Martha came upon Katharine lingering by the boathouse and whispering, "O turtle?" to the evening dews and damps.

"Don't," said Martha. "He won't come. Or if he does," she went on, wisely for her age, "it'll be when we least expect it. He likes a surprise, I think."

One good thing was that Mr. Smith's bookshop didn't seem to be actually failing yet. From a hint garnered here and a remark gleaned there, the four children gathered that business wasn't getting any better, but it wasn't getting any worse, either.

And as August ripened into September, and goldenrod gilded the roadsides and the pollen drifted from the ragweed and Mark began sneezing with his annual hay fever, the thought of magic retreated deep into their minds, and the thought that lay uppermost was the thought of school.

"Only three more days of vacation!" said Martha one sunny afternoon. "Monday's Labor Day. We drive home then."

"O day of labor rightly named!" said Jane. "I think it's mean of them, calling it that. As if going back into bondage weren't bad enough, without rubbing it in!"

"I'm kind of looking forward to next year," said Katharine. "We get fractions."

"Just wait is all I can say!" said Jane.

"What'll we do in the meantime?" said Martha. "We

ought to make every second count. What'll we do today?"

"Get out the rowboat," said Mark.

"Boring." Jane vetoed this. "I know every inch of this shore backwards by now."

"I wasn't thinking of *this* shore so much," said Mark. "I was thinking of the other one." And he pointed across the lake.

"We're not allowed," Katharine reminded him. "They've never found bottom. We're supposed to stay in close to the edge."

"Well?" said Mark. "We don't have to go straight across, do we? We can stay by the edge and row right *around*. I've always been going to do that. And I was thinking. Remember that old broken-down cottage you can see from the *Willa Mae*? The one that looks haunted?"

The mention of this entrancing word was all that was needed to lend a sparkle to every eye and fleetness to every foot. It was a race to see who could reach the boathouse first. Mark won, hotly contested by Jane. Ten minutes later, oars were plying gaily in the direction of Cold Springs.

And soon that gracious center of civilization glided past and into their lee, and they were plowing unfamiliar waters. At least, they'd seen this coast before from the *Willa Mae* dozens of times, but a coast is always different and more interesting when you're up close by it and can note every stone and bush and inch of flaking paint on land.

At first there were just more cottages to note, and laundry hanging out, and tin Lizzies parked in dooryards, and an occasional voice calling something mundane like "We ain't got no eggs." But then the cottages dwindled, and there were desolate tangled thickets, and swamps, and reedy marges, and haunts of coot and hern, as Katharine poetically put it.

Once the rowers, who happened to be Jane and Martha at the moment, were lured off course and found themselves progressing up a stream that got narrower and narrower every minute.

"This must be the lake's source!" said Jane. "We could follow it and dam it up and then see how long it takes the lake to dry!"

"There's no time," said Mark. "Even if there isn't a spring in the bottom, it'd take weeks to evaporate, and we'd be gone home by then and never know. And anyway, I want to see that haunted house. Here, let me."

And he took Martha's oar from her and backed water, and got the boat half turned around, and then they stuck on a mudbank, and time was wasted in recrimination, but at last they were headed the other way, and out into the lake again, and this time it was only a few moments before the weed-clad inlet came into view, with the dilapidated cottage crumbling on its banks.

To beach the rowboat and leap to shore was the work of a moment, and only Martha's feet got *really* wet in the process. The four children scrambled up the stony ledge to where the cottage's front porch sagged from its foundation.

"That way's too dangerous," said Mark. "Let's try around at the back."

Around at the back the kitchen steps still held, and Mark ran up them and the others followed. They stood looking into a murky waste of dust and old newspapers and broken kitchen chairs.

"Come, ghoulie, come, ghaestie, come long-leggedy beastie," said Jane, and a large spider scuttled across the floor. This made a promising start.

They entered the house warily, Katharine and Martha hanging back and clutching at each other. But when no bloodcurdling yells or sheeted forms materialized, they gained courage, and soon were running eagerly from room to room looking for bloodstains on the floor or muffled shapes hiding in closets.

Neither of these proved prevalent, but Martha picked up an old collar button with some dark marks on it that were probably only rust, and Katharine found a scrap of letter that said, "Dear Bert, yours received and contents noted."

And then, as might have been expected, Mark lagged behind the others and hid in a cupboard and didn't answer when they called him, and then started shuffling along the dark hallway after them, and groaning and dragging his feet and clanking a piece of old tire chain he had found. And even though the three girls were almost sure it was Mark all along, they all cried out and gibbered and rushed screaming from the house, and Mark ran howling horribly after them until they all four collapsed breathlessly on the ground of the weedy backyard, amid the shrieks and thudding hearts of utter terror and enjoyment.

"Ow!" said Martha, rubbing herself. "I sat down on something hard."

"A rock, most likely," said Mark, rolling over to investigate. He cleared the encircling weeds away. Then he gulped.

It was a loud gulp, and the others crowded round to see. There, on the ground, lay a flat stone they had seen before. It had initials carved on it. The initials were "C.C." Nobody needed to be told whose initials they were.

"Chauncey Cutlass!" breathed Jane.

"Is it a quincidence?" said Katharine.

"Of course not! It couldn't be! It's *it!* It's the pirate treasure after all these weeks! It's that turtle! It put it there!" cried Jane.

"Sure, don't you see?" said Mark. "This is the one way we could find buried treasure without telling about the magic, and no questions asked! Wasn't that crafty of it?"

"Well? What are we standing here for? Let's be digging," said Katharine.

"Wait," said Mark, and then stopped, thinking hard and fast. "Look. We want Mr. Smith to have the treasure, don't we?"

Three heads nodded.

"Well, then I think *he*'d better be the one that finds it. If *we* dig it up and try to give it to him, he's sure to go all noble and refuse to accept, and want to put it aside in trust funds for our college education! And we don't want *that* kind of thing happening!"

"Ugh!" said Martha.

"It would just utterly and completely ruin everything!" said Jane.

"Exactly!" said Mark. "No. The thing is to leave it, and then lure him here tomorrow, when he's home for the week end, and let nature take its course!"

"Can't we even peek first?" said Katharine.

"It would be leading us into temptation," said Mark.

**174**

"What if somebody finds it and steals it before then?" said Jane.

"I don't think there's much danger," said Mark. "I think it was put there specially for *us*. It's that last wish we made come really true after all. If anybody else happened along, I don't think it'd even exist!"

But he smoothed the attendant weeds back over the stone, just the same.

And regretfully the girls allowed themselves to be led away from the yard and the stone and the haunted house (though *it* had lost all charm by now), and the four children got into the rowboat and headed for home.

No one watched the shore on the journey back, for all hearts burned with impatience to get to the cottage and start working on Mr. Smith. And at last their own beach came in sight, and because it hadn't been a magic adventure (strictly speaking), more time had passed than you would believe, as is usually the case when you've been enjoying yourself thoroughly, and supper was already merrily cooking, but Mr. Smith wasn't there. And their mother told them that a message had been delivered at the farm where the milk came from (for the cottage itself had no telephone). The message was that Mr. Smith had been detained in town on business and wouldn't be home till next day.

And the next day he didn't get there till nearly dark, and it was too late to start luring him anywhere.

"What do you suppose he's been *doing?*" said Martha that night, when four pajamaed forms had assembled upon the sleeping porch. "Do you suppose he's ruined and bankrupt *already?*"

"He can't be," said Katharine. "Not with rescue staring him in the face, if he'd only look."

"I still worry about what's happening to the treasure in the meantime," said Jane. "It might corrode."

"It won't, though," said Mark. "It's all going to work out. It'll have to be tomorrow, though. It's our last day. It's our last chance."

But when they woke up next morning, their mother was already up and heaving bedclothes off beds, and Mr. Smith was in the kitchen packing saucepans into grocery cartons, and all the four children's luring fell upon deaf ears.

"There's just one thing for it," said Jane. "We'll just have to be useful."

And the others privately agreed.

And they worked so hard and fast, and dropped so many hints in between chores, that the unknowing grownups finally got the idea, and their mother finally said, "Everybody's being so good, I think we all deserve a last treat," just as they had willed her to.

And though a visit to a haunted house wasn't perhaps the treat the grownups would have chosen, still, as Mr. Smith said, this was supposed to be the children's summer, and they ought to have the say.

The car was packed now, and the cottage swept clean of all familiarity, except for the bathing suits still hanging on the line. Mr. Smith had decided they would drive home that night to avoid Labor Day traffic next day.

"We'll have a picnic lunch at your haunted house, come back here for a last swim, and then have dinner at the hotel before we go," their mother decided.

Five minutes later they set out, Jane and Mr. Smith leading the way dashingly in the canoe, and Mark and their mother and Katharine and Martha following in the rowboat.

The haunted house was there waiting. And because the four children didn't want to be too obvious about the treasure, they had to pretend to be scared all over again, though it was an old story. And then they warmed to the spirit of the thing and hid in a closet and pounced out, and their mother obligingly shrieked a couple of times, and then it was time for lunch.

The four children chose the spot for the picnic, though their mother suggested other, less weedy, places. Jane and Katharine spread the picnic tablecloth. Mark maneuvered it so Mr. Smith would sit in just the right place. Martha watched with bated breath.

Mr. Smith sat down. Then he looked surprised. Then he looked beneath him.

"Hmmmm," he said. "This is interesting."

"Yes, isn't it?" said Mark unguardedly. Then he remembered and quickly bent over to look at the stone, just as though he hadn't seen it before.

"C.C.," said Mr. Smith, reading the initials. "That must stand for old Mr. Cattermole. He used to live here. They were telling me about him at the hotel the other day."

"No it doesn't," said Martha. "It stands for . . ."

"Shush," said Katharine.

"Well?" said Jane impatiently. "Aren't you going to dig? Aren't you going to find out what's under it?"

"I don't suppose there's anything," said Mr. Smith. "He was a peculiar old man. Proud of anything that was his. Used to put his initials all over everything. Some people said he was a miser. They never found any money after he died, though."

"He *was?* They *didn't?*" said all four children. Their fingers were itching. What they were itching to do shone in their eyes.

"You might as well humor them, Hugo," said their mother, with a long-suffering sigh.

And Mr. Smith began to dig.

"Wasn't that *clever* of the turtle?" said Katharine some time later, as they lay on the beach after their last swim. "Changing the pirate's treasure into good old American ten-dollar bills right before our eyes! And so *many* of them!"

"What *I* don't see," said Jane, "is how he arranged it so old Miser Cattermole had lived there in the first place."

"That turtle moves in a mysterious way," agreed Mark admiringly.

Of course, they weren't going to get the money right away. It seemed that there were rules about buried treasures, just as there were about magic.

"And about just about everything, I guess!" sighed Jane resignedly.

First they had to advertise for old Mr. Cattermole's heirs. And if none turned up, and everybody at Cold Springs seemed to think none would, then the government had to get a lot of it.

"Not that I begrudge *that* part," said Jane. "I'm happy to do my bit."

"You mean Mr. Smith's bit," said Mark.

And it was going to be all right about the bookshop, anyway. Because what had kept Mr. Smith in town was that a man had turned up who thought Toledo, Ohio, *needed* a bookshop, and he was willing to invest some money to make Mr. Smith's bookshop a *bigger* bookshop.

"And even that didn't happen till after we found the treasure," said Mark. "I checked on the time. So you see the turtle did it all."

And if any of the miser's money *did* come to Mr. Smith, he was going to buy a summer cottage with it, so they could have a summer by a lake every year. Only not *this* cottage, because it wasn't for sale.

"And I hope not this lake, either," said Jane. "It would only remind us."

"You're thinking what I'm thinking," said Mark.

"Yes," said Jane. "No more magic for us. It stands to reason. Some people never get any at all, and we've had it twice."

"*Three*'s the magic number," said Katharine wistfully.

"Even so," said Jane firmly, "and notwithstanding."

And in spite of their greedy youth, Katharine and Martha had to agree.

"The only thing that bothers me," said Katharine, "is I thought we'd get to talk to the turtle one more time. I wanted to thank him."

"And *I*," said Martha, "wanted to ask about those three children we met. I liked them."

There was a pause.

"Children!" called their mother. "Time to go!"

The four children got up. They stood looking at the darkening water.

"I'm going to miss this lake," Mark said.

"Another one just won't be the same," Jane agreed.

"If anybody ever plays 'Back Home in Indiana,' again," said Katharine, "I shall cry."

"It'll be better to start fresh, though," said Jane. "Next year."

And the three of them turned their backs on the lake and started for the car.

Martha lingered. She went close to the rippling edge. "O turtle?" she said softly. She waited, listening.

There was a tiny plashing sound, and a head and two front feet appeared where the water joined the land, with a humped shell behind them.

"Well?" said a cold voice.

"Don't worry," said Martha quickly. "I understand about probably no more magic, and I'm not asking for anything more. I just wondered. About those children we met. That Roger and that Ann. I just wondered, will we ever see them again?"

The turtle blinked once. It put out its tongue after a passing midge. Then it spoke. "Time will tell," it said.

Martha's heart beat faster. "Oh, good," she said. "In books that's always a good sign. At least it's better than no."

"But whether you'll know them or not, if you do," went on the turtle, "is another story." It took a backward step, and the waters closed over its head.

Martha stood on the darkling sand thinking this out.

The horn of the car sounded.

"I'm coming!" she called. She ran up the bank toward it.

The car door slammed. The car lights swung round the driveway. There was a pause, as Mark opened the gate into the field. Then the lights moved on up the hill and out of sight.

The waters of the lake plashed softly against the sand. But nobody was there to hear them now.